He gave her a l

"That's what I want... ...were too busy," Nick said.

"Yes, I was." But Maggie wasn't busy now. Now they were on exactly the same page, and the book was about to get very interesting.

He must have been able to read that in her eyes, because his next kiss was different. He still leaned up against the wall, with only his mouth on hers, yet she heated up as though his body was pressed against hers.

"So what were you doing last night that was more important than this?"

Maggie opened her eyes and tried to focus. "It's a secret."

Nick withdrew a little and gave her one of his intense looks.

She snagged the front of his shirt with both hands and pulled him back in. "It's a good secret. When the time is right, I'll tell you all about it."

He seemed to relax a little. "Promise?"

"Promise."

"Then I'll just have to be patient, won't I?"

Dear Reader,

People often want to know how I come up with ideas for my stories, and for the first time I don't have an answer to that question. All I can tell you is that one day I sat at the computer and Nick and Maggie were clamoring for me to tell their story. Looking back, I suspect Maggie was working a little of her magic on me, the same way she does on the people of Collingwood Station…and on that one special man in her life.

Like Maggie, I'm sure we all want the best for the people we love. But how do we achieve the delicate balance between letting them make their own way in life and trying to share the load with them? At what point does helping become meddling? And what if stepping back will make a bad situation worse? Not easy questions to answer, but one thing is certain. When one person leaps without looking and the other has both feet firmly planted on the ground, we can expect a few laughs and the occasional disaster along the way.

I hope you have as much fun reading this book as I had writing it. Please drop by www.leemckenzie.com for a glass of Maggie's ice-cold lemonade and a warm chocolate chip cookie. Collingwood Station will always have a special place in my heart and I hope you'll visit again when my second book set in Collingwood Station, *With This Ring*, comes out in December 2007.

Lee McKenzie

The Man for Maggie
LEE McKENZIE

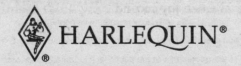

HARLEQUIN®

TORONTO • NEW YORK • LONDON
AMSTERDAM • PARIS • SYDNEY • HAMBURG
STOCKHOLM • ATHENS • TOKYO • MILAN • MADRID
PRAGUE • WARSAW • BUDAPEST • AUCKLAND

ISBN-13: 978-0-373-75171-6
ISBN-10: 0-373-75171-0

THE MAN FOR MAGGIE

www.eHarlequin.com

Printed in U.S.A.

For my family
Thanks for believing

ABOUT THE AUTHOR

From the time she was ten years old and read *Anne of Green Gables* and *Little Women*, Lee McKenzie knew she wanted to be a writer, just like Anne and Jo. In the intervening years she has written everything from advertising copy to an honors thesis in paleontology, but becoming a four-time Golden Heart finalist and a Harlequin author are among her proudest accomplishments. Lee and her artist/teacher husband live on an island along Canada's west coast, and she loves to spend time with two of her best friends—her grown-up children.

Chapter One

Nick Durrance looked at the run-down two-and-a-half-story house and double-checked the address he'd scrawled on a scrap of paper. He'd been surprised—okay, astounded—when his answering service told him that Maggie Meadowcroft wanted an estimate on a remodeling job. Collingwood Station was small enough that there could only be one Miss Meadowcroft. She had been his high-school English teacher, although it had never occurred to him at the time that she had a first name. She'd been positively ancient then, and that had been ten years ago.

Hers was the only house on the block that hadn't been renovated and it definitely needed work. Paint. A new roof. Here's hoping old Miss Meadowcroft had a nice bank account, because he really needed this job.

He pushed the gate open and lunged for it after it swung askew on one hinge. The house also needed new front steps, although to his surprise they held his weight. All but the second step, which looked too risky to chance.

The doorbell had an Out of Order sign taped over it. He added new wiring to the long list forming in his head and knocked on the wooden frame of the screen door.

"Come in!" The voice that beckoned from the back of the house had a husky, musical quality that was utterly feminine and startlingly young. Nothing at all like the Miss Meadowcroft he remembered.

"Wait'll you try this," the voice said. "You'll love it!"

Definitely not Miss Meadowcroft. He gave in to curiosity, pulled the screen door open and stepped inside. The hallway was filled with antiques, many of them much older than the home's owner. He'd have expected the place to be a little on the musty side but instead the air was strangely…fruit-flavored?

"Come on in!" she called again.

The scent of strawberries and that fascinating voice enticed him down the hall to the kitchen. The voice that had conjured up a sultry, mysterious woman actually belonged to a slender redhead who sat at the kitchen table, gazing into a mirror propped against a canister. She was scraping some kind of creamy pink stuff out of a blender with a spatula and smearing it all over her face.

She dumped the spatula back in the blender, spread the stuff around with her fingers and spoke without looking up. "I finally got it right. You will not believe how good this feels."

She popped the tip of one finger between a pair of very luscious-looking lips. "It even tastes—" She glanced up then. "Oh! You're not Allison."

He watched her grab for the nearest kitchen implement and smiled when she ended up arming herself with a wooden spoon.

"Who are you?" she asked. "How did you get in here?"

"Nick Durrance. Through the front door. It wasn't locked and you did say I should come in."

"I thought you were Allison."

"I think we've already established that I'm not."

She glared at him and he chided himself for being a smart-ass. Let's face it. Most women would be surprised to look up and find a six-foot-four construction worker standing in their kitchen.

She pointed her weapon at him. "Allison lives next door. I

called her to come over and test my new rejuvenating pore-cleansing facial mask. She'll be here any minute."

The corners of his mouth twitched and he had to cover them with his thumb and forefinger to make them behave. He understood she was startled but she looked perfectly ridiculous. A pencil protruded from the untidy bundle of dark red hair piled on top of her head and almond-shaped brown eyes gazed suspiciously from two circles in the pink stuff she'd smeared on her face. What man in his right mind would attack a woman who looked like this?

"Listen. I didn't mean to startle you." He took a step forward, and she jumped to her feet and jabbed the wooden spoon in his direction.

"Watch it, mister. I've taken self-defense classes."

He found that difficult to believe. From the neck up, she looked like a cross between Wilma Flintstone and Lucille Ball on a bad-everything day, but from the neck down... whoa! Even faded denim shorts, a purple tie-dyed T-shirt and a string of pearls couldn't disguise a body that just wouldn't...

Wait a minute. Pearls? Who wore pearls anymore? Even his mother had abandoned hers for the kind of bling that Hollywood types wore these days. Apparently pearls were passé. Maybe too reminiscent of the dutiful wife who greeted her husband at the door at the end of the day with a sweet smile and a whiskey sour.

One thing was for sure. This woman was no June Cleaver. If the state of the kitchen was anything to go by, she'd created her rejuvenating cream from yogurt and an assortment of fruit that she'd whipped up in a blender, resulting in the fruit salad scent that had drawn him down the hallway. That, and the voice that felt like the hot-rock massage he'd once experienced at the hands of an even hotter little masseuse whose fear of commitment matched his own. Not that he'd wanted her to commit. He'd wanted her to pay for the work he'd done for her. She'd had other ideas.

"I'm sure your friend is eager to have her grocery store facial but I'm here to see Miss Meadowcroft, so if you could—"

"I'm Miss Meadowcroft." She still stared at him warily but lowered the spoon a few notches.

"Are you?" This time he let the corners of his mouth have their way. "Then I have to tell you, that miracle product of yours really seems to work. You look much younger than the last time I saw you."

She laughed at that. Not the contrived halfhearted giggle that masqueraded as laughter in so many women. Hers was deep and exuberant and it flowed over him like honey on warm toast.

"I'm her niece," she said. "Her great-niece, actually. Miss Maggie Meadowcroft, makeover specialist."

"I see. Is Miss Meadowcroft—retired high-school English teacher and tormentor of teenage boys—here?"

She went serious. "You were one of Aunt Margaret's students? She did have a way of always making you want to try harder, didn't she? To do better."

That was one way to put it. "I wasn't one of her 'do better' students, but apparently she wants to renovate this place, and that's something I can do." Although Shakespeare was still way beyond him, he'd like to show Miss Margaret Meadowcroft that he was good at something.

Maggie tipped her head to one side and looked him up and down, taking her time about it. "I'll bet you're a Capricorn. Determined, distrustful, a little on the cynical side."

"So I've been told. It takes most people longer to figure it out though."

She smiled again. "I knew it. I have a kind of sixth sense about these things."

Give me a break. "Listen, is your aunt—" Some of the yogurty goop dripped off her chin and plopped onto the worn linoleum.

She laughed again. "Oops! I'm dribbling."

He grabbed a towel off the back of a kitchen chair and tossed it to her.

"Thanks. I'll go wash this stuff off." She flung the wooden spoon onto the table and dashed out, holding the towel under her chin.

She was back in less than two minutes and all Nick could do was stare. Why would anyone cover such a beautiful face with…food?

"Is something wrong?" she asked.

"No. No, everything's fine. I should probably talk to your aunt though."

Her eyes went moist. "Aunt Margaret died six months ago."

Add clueless to his list of Capricornian flaws. "Sorry. I didn't know."

She grabbed a tissue out of a box on the table and wiped her eyes. "It was a heart attack—quick as could be, the doctor said. She didn't suffer at all. I still miss her like crazy but she's in a happy place now so I try not to feel badly for her."

A "happy place"? How was he supposed to respond to that? She talked as though she had some kind of inside information.

She brightened a little. "She left everything to me. That's pretty wonderful, don't you think?"

Wonderful for his bank balance. "So, you want to renovate this place?"

"Yes. Lucky for me she left enough money for me to fix up the house *and* start my business."

Lucky. So why was his conscience niggling at him? "It's going to need a lot of work. I think it should be rewired and it definitely needs a new roof. You know, you could always sell it and buy yourself a nice condo."

"A condo?"

He might as well have suggested she cut off an arm.

"I don't think you understand," she said. "I don't just want to live here. I'm going to open a day spa and do natural makeovers. It'll be called Inner Beauty." She smiled up him. "'Making the most of what you've got, naturally.' That's my advertising slogan. What do you think?"

"Catchy."

"I thought so, too! Most spas just work on the person's external appearance but I do makeovers from the inside out. If a person feels good about themselves, then they're naturally beautiful. You know what I mean?"

He didn't have a clue.

"Everyone's always said I have a way with people. Even Aunt Margaret thought so." She waved a hand around the kitchen. "This will be my workspace where I'll create all my beauty products." She ran a hand over her cheek. "Like my rejuvenating pore-cleansing facial mask. It works like a dream. Feel."

She wanted him to touch her? No way.

"Go ahead." She took his hand and guided it to her face. "Amazing, huh?"

Their gazes locked and for a few seconds, maybe longer, he couldn't answer. Amazing indeed.

She leaned closer. "Would you like to try some?" She smelled like strawberries and cream.

He snatched his hand out of hers and stepped back. "No. Thanks. I think we better stick to business."

Her smile suggested she could see right through him. "I'll also need to use the kitchen for making meals because I plan to live upstairs. There are three bedrooms so I'll have lots of space. Come on, I'll show you."

He followed her down the short hallway.

"The spa will be here, in the living room and dining room. I'll need a divider or something to make a change room. I want to put a massage table over there and lots of plants. Over here

I'll have one of those chairs that can be raised and lowered and a big mirror. I want to keep the fireplace, of course, and these wonderful old light fixtures, and most of the antiques and…"

She paused and he thought it was to catch her breath until he saw that her eyes had filled with tears. Aw, jeez. He wasn't good with weepy women. He grabbed a box of tissues off a side table and handed it to her.

"Thanks." She dried her eyes and gave her nose a healthy blow. "I've only been here for a week and all this stuff still makes me kind of emotional." She took a deep breath. "I was going to say that I want to keep the photographs on this wall. Family is so important, don't you think?"

How to answer that? Truthfully, or tell her what she wanted to hear? But then she was talking again, so it didn't matter what he thought.

"I love looking at these old portraits. That's Aunt Margaret and my grandfather. They were brother and sister. My grandparents died ten years ago, three weeks apart. Don't you think that's romantic? Grandma went first, then poor Grandpa died of a broken heart."

Nick bet that's not what the death certificate said.

"My father died in a car accident on my sixteenth birthday. Since then, it's just been me and my mother. And Aunt Margaret, of course. My mother still lives in Greenwich Village. You know, in New York."

Yes, even a small-town guy from Connecticut knew about Greenwich Village, and finding out that's where she came from was no surprise.

"I love the city but now that Aunt Margaret's gone and this house is mine, I can finally open my spa. So you see, I can't possibly sell it."

Right. And he now had way too much information. Never mind that the people of Collingwood Station would look down their aristocratic noses at someone doing natural makeovers. She could always sell the place and go back to the city after this crazy business scheme failed. "So, about the renovations. Do you just want the interior refinished? What about the roof and the wiring?"

The look she gave him was wide-eyed and innocent. "Since you're a former student of Aunt Margaret's, I'm sure I can trust you. If she thinks you're the wrong person for the job, she'll give me a sign."

A sign? From old Miss Meadowcroft? For a few seconds he had a strange feeling that a bolt of lightening was about to strike him. Dead aunts didn't have that kind of power, did they? Oh, man. He must be losing it. "Tell you what. I'll come by first thing tomorrow, do a full inspection and give you a quote for everything that needs to be done. You can look it over and decide if you'd like to hire me and what you want me to do."

Best to leave the dear old aunt out of the equation. Back in high school, he'd been a bad student with a bad attitude and an even badder GPA. The Miss Meadowcroft who'd made his high-school career a living hell wouldn't have trusted him anywhere near her home. And who could blame her? But she was now among the dearly departed and he did not believe in signs from above or beyond or wherever. Business was business.

"Tomorrow will be perfect. What time—"

The screen door squeaked open, taking them both by surprise.

"Hello-o? Sorry it took me so long to get here."

The voice was too real to belong to a spirit. It sounded more like…

No. No way.

Allison Peters. Or Allison Fontaine, if she was using her husband's name. It hadn't occurred to him that *this* was the Allison that Maggie had been talking about, since it was hard to imagine two people who had less in common.

"What did I tell you?" Maggie asked. "This is my friend Allison."

Go figure. Who would have guessed Allison would befriend someone who wore tie-dye?

Nick watched Maggie embrace the woman from his distant past and hoped the past didn't come back to haunt him.

"I'd like you to meet Nick Durrance," she said. "He's a contractor and we've been talking about renovating the house."

For a minute it looked as though Allison might go along with the introduction and pretend she didn't know him. Then she seemed to decide against it. Probably just as well, since it wouldn't take long for Maggie and her sixth sense—with the help of the local gossips—to figure out the truth.

"Nick and I already know each other," Allison said, although she didn't seem to want to look at him. "Sorry I'm late. I waited until John came home from the office so he could stay with the kids."

"How do you two know each other?" Maggie asked.

Nick cleared his throat.

Allison shot him a quick glance and looked away. God, he couldn't believe she was blushing. After all these years…

Maggie grinned. "Ah, I see. Does John know about this?"

"How is John?" he asked, since he was pretty sure Allison would want to avoid Maggie's question.

"Very well, thank you. The kids are fine, too. Oh, and—" she hiked up her chin " John's just made senior partner, but I'm sure your sister told you."

"I guess she forgot to mention it." Which wasn't exactly true. She hadn't mentioned it because she never talked to him, and Allison damned well knew it. "I'm glad you managed to get your lawyer, after all."

"John is a great husband. And father."

"Congratulate him for me."

She eyed him suspiciously.

"On making senior partner."

"Oh. Of course."

Maggie, he could see, was watching the exchange with a lot more interest than the situation merited. After all, he and Allison were ancient history. Prehistoric ancient history. She'd spent their senior year trying to make him into someone he wasn't. When it hadn't worked, she'd gone off to college and by Christmastime that year, she and John Fontaine were engaged.

He took a card out of the back pocket of his jeans and handed it to Maggie. "I'll let you ladies get on with your makeovers. I'll be back in the morning to start on that estimate. Meanwhile, if you think of anything else, Miss Meadowcroft, give me a call."

He headed for the front door, uncomfortably aware of two pairs of eyes on his back.

Chapter Two

The finest-looking rear end Maggie Meadowcroft had ever seen had just walked out the front door and she hadn't done anything to stop it.

Stop him.

Right. As if a man like him would ever be interested in a woman like her. Besides, he'd be back in the morning to give this old house a good going-over. She finally had the place and the money to make her dream come true—and now she had the world's sexiest contractor to help her do it! She couldn't wait to find out more about him, so it was a lucky thing Allison had shown up when she did. Who would know more than an ex-girlfriend?

"It's great that you could come over," Maggie said. "I know how busy you are with the kids and everything."

"Don't be silly. That conditioner you gave me the other day is incredible. My hair has never felt softer."

"I'm glad you liked it." Why was everyone always so amazed that natural products were, well, more natural?

Natural or not, Allison looked fabulous. How the woman did it, Maggie would never know. She took care of that big house, her husband and two kids and she always looked liked a cover model. Never a hair out of place. Beautiful clothes. Make that beautiful, *expensive* clothes.

Maggie would always remember her mother's reaction when she'd admired a dress in the window of an exclusive shop on the Upper East Side. "Designer clothes will make anyone look good, Maggie, but they don't change how a person feels about herself. That's something that comes from the heart."

She fingered the string of pearls around her neck. Her mother was a wise woman. "Come on into the kitchen," she said to Allison. "I'm dying to have you try my new mask. It's pure heaven."

She seated Allison at the kitchen table and draped a plastic cape over her shoulders. It was one thing to spill this stuff on herself, but ruining Allison's silk shirt would not be good. "So," she said, trying to sound casual, "Nick Durrance is a friend of yours?"

"Not anymore. We dated in high school. Of course, at the time I was convinced he was 'the one.' I did my best to help him get his life on track but some men just can't be changed."

"Hmm. There's no doubt he'd make an interesting project," Maggie said, as much to herself as to Allison. She brushed Allison's hair away from her face and clipped it in place.

"Trust me. Nick is way beyond help. His mother and his sister—even his grandmother—have all tried. God knows, I did. He breaks the heart of every woman who tries to reform him."

Silly women, Maggie thought. That wasn't the kind of project she had in mind. "Are you wearing makeup?" she asked.

Allison shook her head. "On the phone you said you wanted to try out a mask, so I thought I should take it off. I can't imagine what Nick must have thought, seeing me like this."

That you look as beautiful as ever? "So, tell me about you and Nick," she said instead.

"There's nothing to tell," Allison said a little too quickly.

"Does John know you dated him?"

"Of course. We all went to high school together."

"I see." What would Nick have been like back then? Oh!

Aunt Margaret had a whole collection of Collingwood High School yearbooks upstairs. "When did you graduate?" she asked casually, applying an even layer of the strawberry mask to Allison's forehead.

"It seems like so long ago. We just had our ten-year reunion. Of course, Nick didn't bother to show up."

Interesting. That meant he was about four years older than she was. She smoothed the mask over the rest of Allison's face.

"What's this stuff made of?" Allison asked. "It smells good enough to eat."

"Well, it is edible. I really believe that what we put *on* our bodies is as important as what we put *in* them."

Maggie set the container in the sink and filled it with water. To be totally effective, the mask should stay on for fifteen minutes. She set the timer for ten. She could hardly wait to get Allison out of here so she could go upstairs to find that yearbook.

"Are you comfortable?" she asked.

"I'm fine."

"These kitchen chairs are pretty unforgiving. I'll have one of those nice adjustable, reclining chairs in the spa."

Allison smiled. "How did you come up with this idea?"

"I'm not sure, exactly." She climbed onto a stool and hooked her heels on the top rung. "I've wanted to do this for as long as I can remember but I couldn't afford to rent a shop in New York."

"Did you live there all your life?"

Maggie nodded. "Yes, my whole life. My mother lives in the Village. My father was a musician and she is a…" How would Allison react to the truth? Only one way to find out. "She does readings."

"Oh. You mean, she's a writer? A poet?" Allison actually sounded interested.

Maggie shook her head. "She's a clairvoyant."

Silence. "I see," she said finally.

Maggie very much doubted she did, since she couldn't imagine Allison ever consulting one. "She's very good. She even helped the N.Y.P.D. solve a missing persons case."

Allison perked up a little. "Oh, now that is amazing. I've heard about people who can do that. I'd love to meet her sometime."

"Oh, I'm sure you will. Gabriella hates leaving the city but now that I'm living here, she's bound to visit once in a while." But try as she might, she couldn't imagine her outlandish mother and her straitlaced neighbor having anything in common. "Tell me more about you and Nick…and John, of course…when you were in high school."

But apparently Allison didn't want to reminisce. "Are you really going to hire him to renovate this place?" she asked.

"Would it cause problems for you and John if he's working here?"

"Not at all. Don't be silly."

But Maggie saw the color creep up Allison's neck. "I like Nick," she said. "He seems to know a lot about renovating old houses, but he wants to give me an estimate before I make a decision."

Allison's eyes widened. "I should hope so. Don't let him take advantage of you."

What a strange thing for her to say. "I'm a very good judge of character and I can't see him doing that."

Pencil-thin eyebrows arched beneath the pink mask.

"It's true," Maggie said. "I can tell he's honest, but for some reason he's not happy." And although he was about as good-looking as a guy could be, he didn't seem to have a lot of confidence when it came to women. In spite of her track record with men, she'd like to think she could fix that. "You know, I envy you."

"Me? Why?" But Allison did not sound surprised.

"You've been in love twice. Well, twice that I know of."

"Are you saying you're interested in Nick?"

"No! I just met him. All I'm saying that being in love twice, first with Nick and then with John…do you know how lucky that is?"

Allison suddenly seemed preoccupied with the cuticle of one perfectly manicured nail. "Are you saying you've never fallen in love?"

"Oh, yes, I've *fallen* in love, but I've never *been* in love with anyone."

Allison looked up at her. "There's a difference?"

"Of course. I've fallen in love twice. Three times if you count sixth grade, but I don't. I'm pretty sure I was too young. But I fell seriously in love when I was a senior, with a boy who didn't even know I was alive." Her insides startled her by contracting unexpectedly. Nick reminded her of that boy. Jeremy… Hmm. She couldn't believe she'd forgotten his name.

"And the second time?"

"The second time was when I moved into my own apartment and became friends with the guy across the hall."

"But?"

"Just when I started to think he might fall in love with me, a woman named Debbie moved into the apartment down the hall. Six months later he asked her to marry him. So although I've *fallen* in love, I've never *been* in love with someone who loved me back."

"That's an interesting distinction. I've never thought of it that way."

Yeah, well, Allison had probably had dozens of boys—and men—fall in love with her, so the odds were that she was bound to love some of them back.

Maggie sighed. "Someone fell in love with me once, in high school. He was so sweet and I did everything in my power to fall in love with him, but nothing worked. I even begged my mother to cast one of her spells on us, but she said a love spell would only work if love was destined to be. In my case, she was sure it wasn't, and, of course, she was right."

"Your mother does love spells?"

Watch what you say around these people, Maggie.

Aunt Margaret? Is that you?

Allison was watching her, waiting for an answer.

Now that she'd blurted the stuff about love spells, she couldn't think of a way out of it. "Yes, she does. But apparently there's nothing she can do to help me. I have a habit of falling in love with the wrong men. Not bad men—" she hastened to add "—just men who don't fall in love with women like me."

"And what kind of woman are you, Maggie Meadowcroft?"

"Me?"

Watch what you say around these people.

"Well, let's see. I have a tendency to leap before I look. I always have good intentions, but sometimes I rush into things and they don't always turn out the way I planned."

There, that sounded safe enough.

"You'll fall in love someday, Maggie, and when it happens, it will have been worth the wait. But—" she studied her cuticle some more "—just a word of advice. You mentioned falling for the wrong ones. Nick's one of them."

Maggie jumped down from the stool and started to clear things off the kitchen table. "I'm sure you're right." She wanted to say, "Give me a little credit." She might be impulsive, but she always learned from experience. Nick Durrance was definitely one of the many, *many* men who would never fall in love with her.

But she could be curious, couldn't she?

She decided to change the subject. "Nick said Aunt Margaret was his English teacher. Were you in her class, too?"

Allison seemed to relax a little. "Yes. And trust me, she could have told you stories about Nick Durrance."

"Really?" *Note to self. Find out what Aunt Margaret thinks of him now.*

"Miss Meadowcroft loved Shakespeare," Allison said. "Of course, you probably know that."

"Yes. *Hamlet* was her favorite. Whenever she suspected I was up to something, she'd say 'Maggie Meadowcroft, something's rotten in the state of Denmark.' It was years before I understood what that meant. I used to imagine Denmark filled with piles of rotting garbage. Kind of like New York one summer when the garbage collectors were on strike."

Allison gave her an odd look. "I doubt that Nick ever tried to figure out Shakespeare. He spent more time in detention than in English class. Or any class, for that matter."

That opinion seemed grossly unfair. Shakespeare wasn't for everyone. Just like not everyone could renovate a house. "He must have been good at something."

"Nick was very charming in those days and he didn't take anything, or anyone, seriously. Not even himself. From what his sister tells me, that hasn't changed."

Everyone had strengths and positive traits. Maggie couldn't tell if Allison had ignored her point, or if she just didn't get it. She decided to try a different line of questioning. "You mentioned his family. What are they like?"

"You haven't heard of the Durrance family?"

"Hmm. No, I don't think so."

"I thought you used to spend summers up here with your aunt."

"I did, but she wasn't into…" *Gossip.* "Um, she made a point of not talking about her students."

"That makes sense. Nick's father was a judge and so was his grandfather. Everybody assumed Nick would go into law, too. He was at the top of the class when we were freshman, then overnight everything changed."

"How strange. What do you think happened?"

Allison shrugged. "Well, his father died. It was totally un-expected, but still, most people get over things like that. But it seemed to turn Nick into a different person and he never got back to normal."

Hello? A young, teenage boy lost his father and everyone expected him to just "get over it"? Maggie had only been a little older when her father died. She'd missed him like crazy, but on another level, he'd still been there with her and her mother. That was when she'd first become aware that she had what Aunt Margaret called "the gift."

"Maybe he really missed his father," she said.

"Anything's possible, but according to Leslie, Judge Dur-rance was a workaholic. He devoted himself to his career and other than having high expectations of her and Nick, he pretty much ignored them."

"Who's Leslie?"

"Nick's sister."

"I see," Maggie said, glancing at the timer. Only a few more minutes. "How does your skin feel?"

"Great. How long does this stay on?"

"Just another minute or two. So, is Leslie older or younger than Nick?"

"A year younger. She's an attorney, just like everyone expected her to be. Probably her mother's influence. Lydia Durrance—Nick's mother—is an amazing woman. She has a beautiful home and she puts on the most incredible garden parties you've ever been to."

Except that Maggie had never been to one. The Village was well-known for its parties, but they weren't the garden variety.

Allison was still gushing. "On top of that, she does a lot for the community. There's even a charity named after her."

"Really? She sounds formidable."

Allison laughed. "She is, in a way."

And yet you'd give almost anything to be her, Maggie thought. *Interesting.*

The timer buzzed. "All right, then. Let's take this off." She gently washed the mask off Allison's face and patted her skin dry. "What do you think?"

Allison ran both hands along the sides of her face. "Amazing. I don't know how you do this with just the stuff in your kitchen."

"Chemical-based products dry your skin and then you need more chemicals to make it moist again. Natural ingredients are all about pampering yourself."

"When you first told me about this idea of yours, I didn't think it would work. Now I can't wait for your spa to open. Will you let me be the first customer?"

Maggie walked her neighbor to the front door. "Sure. Any chance you might tell your friends about it, too?"

Allison smiled one of her rare smiles. "You know, I'm tempted to keep you all to myself."

Maggie laughed. "Then you'd better plan to give me a lot of business!"

Allison gave her an unexpected hug. "I'm glad you moved into your aunt's house, Maggie. Miss Meadowcroft was a nice neighbor, but I think I'm really going to like having you here."

Maggie hugged her back. "What a sweet thing to say. Thank you."

"I'd better get home. John will be wondering what's happened to me and the kids are probably driving him crazy."

"Tell him I said hello." Maggie gently closed the door, then bolted up the stairs to find those yearbooks.

NICK CRACKED OPEN a beer and tossed a frozen dinner into the microwave. After punching a few numbers on the keypad, he leaned against the counter and took a swig from the bottle.

Images of Maggie Meadowcroft and the sound of her silky

smooth voice kept drifting through his mind. She was one intriguing woman. Damned attractive—for all the obvious reasons, of course—and he'd swear she didn't have a pretentious bone in her body. In spite of the pearls.

He tried to picture his mother and sister at a place that served up skin-care products made of yogurt and mayonnaise.

Nope. Couldn't do it.

Nothing but the best for the Durrance women, and everyone knew the best came with a hefty price tag and a designer label. Maggie, on the other hand, wanted to sink her inheritance into converting an old house into a day spa.

What had she called it? Inner Beauty?

Actually he kind of liked the sound of that. It suggested that she intended to work with what a person already had instead of trying to make them into something they weren't. Admirable intentions but not much of a business plan. Especially not for this town, where people like his mother and sister were the rule rather than the exception.

The microwave pinged just as he finished his beer. He grabbed another from the fridge, fished around in the cutlery drawer for a fork and opened the microwave. Using a dish towel as a pot holder, he slid his dinner out and dumped it on the counter before the heat completely pierced the towel.

He shoved the newspaper and three days' worth of mail to the side, pulled the cellophane cover off his dinner and inhaled. Man, he really needed to learn how to cook.

Maggie seemed pretty handy in the kitchen.

But thinking about Maggie was not good. Especially since it looked as though she was about to become a client.

He jabbed the remote, thinking the news or even a sitcom rerun would be preferable to thinking about one very sassy little makeover specialist. Five minutes and twenty channels later, he was still thinking about her. He'd also finished his dinner and was halfway through his second beer. Maybe he should take a look at the mail.

Phone bill.

Credit card application.

Something addressed to "Occupant." He tossed that one straight into the trash.

An ivory vellum envelope. His mother's trademark stationery, addressed in his sister's handwriting. He stared at it, trying to figure out what Leslie might have sent him.

An invitation to someone's birthday? No. His grandmother's birthday was in the fall. So was Leslie's. His mother had just had hers and if there'd been a celebration, he hadn't been invited. He'd sent flowers, though, and a week later had received a stilted thank-you note—in an envelope exactly like this one.

So what could this be? He picked up the envelope, turned it over and studied the flap.

What the hell? Go for it.

It was an invitation to his sister's wedding. He sure couldn't have predicted that.

The inner envelope was addressed to "Nick and Escort." *Great.* They expected him to subject someone to a Durrance family function. On the bright side, they didn't want him to be in the wedding party. And if he worked at it, maybe he could come up with an excuse not to go at all.

He read the card. Leslie was to marry Gerald Bedford III. The third in a succession of stuffed shirts. Nick had only seen them together twice and that was all it had taken to know this was not a match made in heaven. It was, however, the blending of two prominent Collingwood Station families. The wedding would be some shindig and it was taking place three weeks from Saturday. For a moment he speculated on the need to hold a wedding on such short notice. Surely his sister wasn't having a shotgun wedding.

Nah.

Leslie was too cautious and too smart to let anything like that happen.

He slid the invitation under a magnet on the fridge door and snagged another beer while he was there. That's when he noticed the light flashing on the answering machine.

Three messages.

One from a subcontractor.

One from Leslie, sweetly asking if he'd received the invitation, saying how much she looked forward to having him there on her special day and apologizing for the short notice but it was the only time she and Gerald could clear their calendars *and* the only time the country club was available *and* blah, blah, blah.

Poor Leslie. She was too much like their mother for her own good, except she didn't nag as much. Maybe if he'd been around more after their father died, she wouldn't have been so influenced by the family matriarch.

The third message was from the matriarch herself, asking him to inform her, at his earliest convenience, as to the name of his date so she could finalize the seating plan and place cards.

Jeez, Mother. Would you like that in triplicate?

He punched the Delete button.

He stared a minute at the unopened beer in his hand and decided to put it back in the fridge. He'd promised Maggie he'd be there first thing in the morning and he wanted to have a clear head.

He unfolded the newspaper and flipped it open. What he needed was a distraction. A good story about an armed robbery. He turned the page. Murder and mayhem. Another page. The daily horoscope. He rolled his eyes but couldn't resist scanning the list until he came to Capricorn.

Your life will take a surprising turn today. Whether it's business or personal, roll with the punches and you'll reap the rewards. And if you go the extra mile, there could even be a happily-ever-after in your future.

Roll with the punches? Reap the rewards? Who writes this stuff? Come to think of it, though, there had been a few surprises.

Maggie Meadowcroft.

Allison Peters Fontaine.

Leslie's wedding.

As for rolling with the punches, he'd been doing that all his life. But happily-ever-after? Maggie had been the day's only prospect. She was new in town so she wouldn't have heard the mostly unfounded rumors about his bachelor lifestyle. But she also believed in the zodiac and in getting signs from dead people, so in spite of the crazy attraction he'd felt for her, Maggie Meadowcroft was not the woman for him.

So much for horoscopes.

MAGGIE SPRAWLED on the floor of her aunt's guest room with four of Collingwood High's yearbooks spread open in front of her. Nick's freshman photograph had made her laugh. He had a bad haircut, a *Star Wars* T-shirt and a shaky smile. Over the next few years, an interesting transformation had taken place and by his senior year, Nick Durrance was no laughing matter.

He had probably been the high-school crush of every girl at Collingwood High. He would have been the boy they wanted to go to senior prom with and he definitely would have been the boy their fathers wanted them to stay away from.

Allison Fontaine had been Allison Peters in those days. The girl with movie-star hair and a perfect smile. The girl every other girl wanted to be. Their senior write-ups said that Allison's favorite pastime was "taming Nick." Nick's was "breaking hearts."

According to what Allison had said that afternoon, some things never changed. Except the part about her taming Nick, of course. The whole world could see that Allison and John were happily married and very much in love, with a gracious home and two adorable children. They had everything they wanted. And Maggie doubted that John had ever needed taming.

She leaned in for a closer look at Nick. Aunt Margaret's pearls swung forward and she caught them, liking the feel of their smooth coolness between her fingers.

At some point, the sci-fi fan who'd played trombone in the school band had been replaced by a rebel without a cause. If what she'd seen today was anything to go by, the defiance in those dark blue eyes had intensified with time. What had happened during Nick's high-school years? Had his father's death been solely responsible for the transformation?

She looked at Allison's picture again. Maggie hadn't been cool enough or pretty enough to be a cheerleader or prom queen like Allison but that hadn't stopped her from having a wild crush on the hottest guy in school. At the time she'd have given anything to have her heart broken by him. That hadn't happened and if she was careful, it wouldn't happen with Nick, either.

Her family had always told her that she had a gift for being able to see inside people and to bring out the best in them. Sometimes it was frightening. People kept some scary stuff hidden inside. Maybe… Now, there was an interesting thought… Maybe she could help Nick.

Hmm.

"What do you think, Aunt Margaret?"

She waited for an answer, but either her aunt had no comment or she was preoccupied with something else.

Maggie pondered the thought some more and before she knew it, all kinds of ideas were tumbling through her head. Helping Nick discover himself and bringing out all his positive traits was definitely something she could do. Once she got to know his family—and since this was such a small town, their paths were bound to cross—she'd have even more insight into what was keeping him from being happy.

Yes, her plan sounded better and better the more she thought about it.

Nick Durrance, tortured soul. In need of help.

Maggie Meadowcroft, makeover specialist. To the rescue.

Chapter Three

The next morning Maggie was up at dawn, trying to organize her ideas into a coherent state. Nick had said he'd be here "first thing" to work out an estimate for the renovations. They hadn't had the best introduction yesterday. He'd made it clear that he thought she was a flake, and he certainly wasn't the first. She knew her ideas seemed a little strange to some people, but she was more sensible than most gave her credit for being. Really, she was.

She usually didn't care what people thought but she wanted to convince Nick that she knew what she was doing. She needed him to trust her because, whether he knew it or not, they had a lot in common. He didn't conform to others' expectations any better than she did.

He was a Capricorn. She was a Gemini.

Of course, he was a little more down-to-earth and practical. She could be impulsive, even a little rash at times.

While he was absolutely gorgeous, she wasn't exactly the kind of woman who turned heads. Men like Nick were never interested in women like her. The boys in high school had preferred girls like Allison, and it was something they didn't overcome with age. Of course, Nick didn't need to be attracted to her for this makeover to work, but it would help if he liked her.

Or at least trusted her.

A little.

Since yesterday afternoon she'd spent way too much time thinking about him. Studying his yearbook pictures had taken her back to her own high-school days, pining over Jeremy What's-his-name and settling for being Albert "Einstein" Fedoruk's prom date. Why couldn't she have fallen in love with poor Albert? He was now a NASA scientist, which was way more amazing than anything anyone else from her graduating class had done. She had no idea what had become of Jeremy but she hoped he was happier than Nick.

Last night she'd fallen asleep with Nick Durrance on her mind and he'd still been there when she woke up this morning. In between, she'd had one of those dreams that was made up of a collage of bizarre events. Jeremy inviting her to the prom, Albert working on the renovations and a shadowy, ever-present Nick Durrance watching from the sidelines.

She wasn't even going to try to analyze that. Instead she poured herself a second cup of peppermint tea and thought ahead to the renovations.

Once it was fixed up, this stately old home that had been in her family for three generations would give tons of credibility to her and her business. At least she hoped it would. She'd been in town almost a week and had the impression that the prim and proper people of Collingwood Station thought she was a little odd, even for a city girl. Of course, they didn't know the half of it, so she still needed all the credibility she could get.

Someone knocked at the front door.

Nick!

She'd kept the door locked on purpose so he'd have to wait until she opened it for him. There'd be no surprises this morning. She smoothed her hair and opened the door.

Okay, maybe just one surprise.

Nick stood on the front porch with a giant schoolboy grin on his face and a huge basket of fruit in his arms.

"Good morning," she said. "I see you packed a lunch."

His laugh sounded a little nervous. "I guess it's a house-warming gift. I stopped at Donaldson's Deli for coffee and this was sitting on the counter. I figured you can always eat what you don't use for makeup, or whatever."

A huge pineapple sat in the middle of the basket, surrounded by peaches, kiwis, strawberries, oranges, a mango, even a passion fruit, all wrapped up in cellophane and tied with a giant purple bow.

The tears that puddled on her lower eyelids made everything go blurry.

"You're not going to cry again, are you?"

She shook her head and wiped her eyes with the back of her hand. Yesterday, after she'd become emotional about her aunt, he'd almost certainly left thinking she was a bit of a nutcase. This morning she'd been determined to show him that she could be a conventional businesswoman with a well-thought-out business plan, and here she was getting emotional over a basket of fruit.

He finally broke the awkward silence. "It's all organic."

"How did you know I use organic ingredients?"

"Just a hunch."

She finally remembered her manners. "Please come in. And thank you. This is very thoughtful."

He stepped inside, letting the screen door bang shut behind him. He looked exactly the same as he had yesterday—white T-shirt, faded jeans and scuffed work boots. Today he also had a clipboard tucked under his arm and a tape measure hooked on his belt.

She took the basket from him. "I'll just put this in the kitchen." Then she walked down the hallway, thinking how good Nick was going to look in a tool belt, all rugged and work-manlike.

You're crazy, she told herself. *All construction workers wear tool belts and Nick will look just like any other man on a construction site.*

Not.

That's beside the point, she told herself. *You have to be professional.*

She took a deep cleansing breath, closed her eyes and tried to clear her mind by picturing herself in a field of wildflowers.

It didn't work.

Nick stood in the midst of all those flowers, still wearing the blue jeans and tool belt, but the T-shirt was gone. The contours of his bare chest and work-hardened biceps glistened with perspiration.

Her eyes popped open. *No way, Maggie Meadowcroft. This has to stop.* She absolutely could not let herself imagine Nick in that field, or anywhere else, wearing any less clothing.

No matter how much she wanted to.

She closed her eyes again. Okay, maybe one little peek.

"Am I interrupting something?"

Her eyes flew open.

Nick stood in the doorway, holding her sketches and looking a little puzzled about finding her standing in a trance in the middle of the kitchen.

A wave of heat flashed across her face. So much for being professional. "You weren't interrupting anything," she said. "I was just thinking."

"I see."

He didn't say that he wondered what she'd been thinking about. He didn't have to.

"You have sketches. They're very good," he said. "Did you draw them?"

"The sketches? Oh, yes. I wanted to, you know, to get an idea of what should go where and how everything will look when it's finished and…" *For heaven's sake, Maggie. Stop babbling.*

If he thought she was out of her mind, he was too nice to let on. "These are very good drawings."

"Really?"

"Yes. Maybe you should have been an architect."

Maggie Meadowcroft, Architect? "I don't think so. Too many rules and regulations and building codes."

"You don't like rules?"

"Rules are fine but I'm not always very good at following them."

His mouth spread into a wry smile. "Now, why doesn't that surprise me?"

"So you think you've already got me figured out?" she asked.

"Oh, I wouldn't go that far. But take yesterday, for example. You were wearing a tie-dyed T-shirt and pearls." His eyes now held a spark of mischief. "When everyone knows the rules of fashion dictate that rubies should be worn with tie-dye."

She did like a man with a sense of humor. "And how do you know so much about these things?"

The flash of humor disappeared and a hint of the bitterness she'd detected yesterday crept back into his voice. "My mother has single-handedly ensured the success of the jewelry industry."

Interesting. "Those were Aunt Margaret's pearls that I was wearing. I've never had any real jewelry so I wanted to know how it felt to wear them."

"And? How did they make you feel?"

She remembered exactly how she'd felt. "Like a princess. There's something elegant and understated about pearls."

"But you're not wearing them this morning."

"No. They don't go with faded denim, either."

"Oh, I don't know. Princesses must wear blue jeans sometimes."

She tried to strike a regal pose. "Of course we do, but we prefer to wear diamonds with denim."

"I see. I'll remember that."

And she had a feeling he would. She also liked the way his smile made her feel a little light-headed. It sure made it difficult to be professional though. "You must be very busy, running a big construction company and all. Maybe we should talk about the work that has to be done on the house."

"Sure thing."

"Would you like a cup of tea?" she asked. "It's herbal."

He shook his head. "No, thanks. Do you have any coffee?"

"Sorry." But she made a mental note to buy some and figure out how to make it.

He studied the two sketches in his hand and glanced at the others spread on the kitchen table. "You've drawn quite a few different floor plans. Is there one you prefer?"

"Yes. Actually, I like the two you're holding but I can't make up my mind which layout will work best."

"Why don't you explain what you want and we'll take it from there."

She knew exactly what she wanted. His hands were strong and tanned and rough from work. After experimenting with several essential oils and plant extracts, she had found the perfect blend for softening the skin and relaxing tired muscles.

Would he think she was too forward if she suggested a hand massage?

She looked up, straight into those luscious dark eyes. Yes, he probably would.

Take it slow, Maggie, she chided herself. *Once you've hired Nick, you'll have all the time you need to get him to loosen up and reconnect with his feelings.* "I was thinking I'd like to convert the living room into an area for doing hair and facials and set up a massage table in the dining room. What do you think?"

"You do massage?" he asked.

It was a loaded question. "Therapeutic massage. It helps people relax and improves the circulation."

"Right." He lowered his head and studied her drawings some more, almost as though he was seeing them for the first time.

"So what do you think?" she asked.

"About what?"

She pointed to the sketch. "About this arrangement?"

"Oh. Right. Well, it does create an open floor plan but it has a few drawbacks. Do you want a sink here?" he asked, pointing to a corner of the living room.

"Yes. I thought that would be the best place for it. Is that a problem?"

"Not really a problem. Just more expensive. The existing plumbing is at this side of the house." He indicated the kitchen and bathroom. "It would be a lot easier to tie into that if we install the sink in the dining room."

She hadn't given that any thought but she could see it made sense. "Is there a big difference in cost?"

He named a figure and she sucked in a startled breath. "I see. My preference was to put the massage table in the living room, anyway, but with all those windows it's not very private."

He seemed to give that some thought. "We have some old stained-glass windows left over from our last renovation. The owner didn't want them but they seemed too valuable to throw out so we put them in the warehouse. We might be able to make those work. Should give you lots of privacy and still let in plenty of light."

"Really? I'd love that!" She sifted through a pile of papers till she found a folder of fabric swatches and color chips. "Do you remember what color they are?"

He shook his head.

"I don't think it will matter. I plan to use lots of neutral shades—cream and beige with lots of natural wood. And I'll use purple for the accent color. What do you think?"

"I just paint. I don't interior decorate," he told her. "You'll have to get someone else's opinion on colors."

"No problem. I'm pretty sure Allison will help. Her home is beautifully decorated." Although, come to think of it, there wasn't a speck of purple anywhere.

Nick sighed. It was a small sigh but still unmistakable. "Will she be spending a lot of time here?" he asked.

Maggie glanced up and looked straight into his eyes. She was usually so good at reading people but at that moment she had no idea what Nick needed to hear.

"Yes, some," she said, cautiously feeling her way. "I don't know her very well but she's been very nice to me since I moved in. She's busy though, with her kids and her husband and—"

"I wasn't fishing for information. I was hoping you'd say yesterday was a one-shot deal and we'd never see her again."

"Oh."

He set the sketches on the table. "So what did Allison tell you about me?"

Maggie hadn't expected him to be so direct. "Not much. Nothing at all, actually. We were busy trying out the new mask and, of course, she couldn't stay long because she had to get home and make dinner for John and the kids and, well, we didn't really have a chance to talk about you." *Shut up, Maggie. You're babbling again*

Nick folded his arms across his chest and stared at her. "Yeah, right. So why do I get the feeling there's something you're not telling me?"

"Okay, fine. She said she tried to reform you and that you broke her heart." She'd always been a lousy liar. Unfortunately she also had a tendency to blurt the whole truth when only part of the truth was necessary.

He gave his head an exasperated shake. "My father was a lawyer and his father was a lawyer. My little sister is now a lawyer and everyone assumed I'd be a lawyer. Everyone. My parents, my grandmother, my sister. Allison." He gave her a cynical smile. "Come to think of it, though, Miss Meadowcroft seemed to know I wasn't destined for law school."

That poor boy was never allowed to explore his real talents. It's time someone gave him a chance, Maggie, my dear. Aunt Margaret's insights were never a surprise but her unexpected presence caught Maggie off guard.

Most people believed the voices she heard were just her imagination but she knew they were real. Otherwise they wouldn't always be right. "You're good at what you do now, that's what's important. I'm sure your family is very proud of you."

"My family is proud of its longstanding affiliation with this country's justice system. They weren't prepared for a son who made a living by using his hands instead of his head."

Aunt Margaret was right.

And Nick's makeover was about to begin.

By the time he finished renovating her house, she'd have him believing in himself. She picked up the folder of sketches and color samples, already feeling a smug sense of accomplishment. "Maybe we should get back to work."

Two hours later they had measured and remeasured the rooms on the main floor and roughly sketched out a new floor plan. Nick went down to the basement to check the electrical panel and, finally, he listened patiently to her ideas for updating the bathroom.

"I want this room to be really special," she said. "There'll be a separate dressing room here, with a shower and a soaker tub at the far end."

Nick was shaking his head. "Except for one problem. Your sketch isn't to scale. The only soaker tub that'll fit in here will be about the size of your kitchen sink."

She looked at her drawing, then at the bathroom, then back at the drawing. Disappointment set in. "You see? This is why I can't be an architect."

He laughed. "What are your plans for the den?"

"I'd like to use it as an office."

"If we move this wall, you'll still have a small office and there'll be enough space to do the bathroom reno the way you want it."

"You can do that? Just move the wall?"

"Well, there's a little more to it than that. We'll actually have to tear out this wall and build a new one, but it'll only take a day or two."

He said it as though he had no idea how amazing that was. "Let's do it! I only need enough room in the office for a desk and filing cabinet and I really, really, really want this bathroom."

He glanced at his notes and her sketches and took a few more measurements. "I think that's it. I'll redraw these plans to scale and have the estimate ready by tomorrow afternoon."

"When will you be able to start?"

"If you decide to go ahead, I can get some of the materials delivered this week and we should be able to begin on Monday."

"Perfect." She had complete confidence that he'd quote a fair price and she'd already made up her mind to hire him. After all, he needed her as much as she needed him. But it would look more professional if she waited till she saw the estimate before she offered him the job.

She gathered her papers and glanced up at the hall clock. The morning had flown by. Nick had patiently listened to all her ideas and made suggestions when he thought something else would work better. Such as his suggestion for expanding the bathroom. And best of all, he didn't seem to think she was completely crazy for doing this.

"Would you like to stay for lunch? I have stuff for sandwiches and there's lots of fruit for dessert."

He glanced at his watch and at the notes on his clipboard and she fully expected him to say no. Then he looked at her and smiled that heartbreaker smile of his. "Sure. Why not?"

NICK RAN WATER into the ancient pedestal sink in the bathroom and picked up a bar of purple soap. Obviously one of Maggie's creations. He sniffed it suspiciously. Too flowery for his liking but it was all he could find.

Staying for lunch was probably a bad idea, he thought as he dried his hands on a bright red towel. Mixing business with pleasure always seemed to land him in a tight spot.

On the other hand, why shouldn't he stay? Maggie's refreshingly off-the-wall conversation made him laugh, and God knew he didn't usually do a lot of that. She was easy on the eyes and he couldn't remember the last time he'd had lunch with a beautiful woman who wasn't trying to use her looks to get her hooks into him.

He'd also lost count of the number of women who thought he had access to the Durrance fortunes, and who quickly hit the road when they found he didn't. Either Maggie didn't care about the money or she didn't know about it. For now, either option worked.

He found her standing at the kitchen counter, assembling two enormous sandwiches. "Can I help?"

"Sure. There's a pitcher of lemonade in the fridge and glasses in the far cupboard."

He grabbed the glasses and opened the fridge. One shelf was completely filled with labeled plastic containers.

Oatmeal Cleanser.

Banana-Honey Anti-Aging Mask.

Cream of Wheat Body Scrub.

Cream of Wheat? Oh, man. She really was something.

He closed the fridge door, his amusement tempered by pangs of guilt. Ten years ago this neighborhood had been filled with run-down old houses like this one. Thanks to the town council's ambitious program to attract tourists, most of the houses had been restored to their original elegance. Many were still private residences but others had been converted into antique shops, art galleries and cafés. Renovating an old house in this posh neighborhood was a good investment but no matter how he looked at it, converting it into a food-based beauty parlor was the craziest thing he'd ever heard.

It's none of your business, Durrance. She's an adult and she can do whatever she wants with her money. He hated having anyone meddle in his life and he wasn't about to meddle in anyone else's. Although, he was curious how she thought she could make a living at this. And asking a few questions didn't make him a busybody.

He poured the lemonade into the two glasses. "Have you ever heard of one these kinds of spas before? I mean, one that uses fruit and stuff to make...you know...stuff?"

"I've seen them in the city, but I knew Collingwood Station didn't have one. That's what makes it such a good idea."

Interesting logic. "So you really think a natural spa will work here?"

"I'm sure of it," she said, adding sliced tomatoes and carrot sticks to each plate. "Everyone likes to be pampered and to feel they're doing something good for their bodies."

"You're probably right." And if she wasn't, well, it was no concern of his.

"Besides, I have a way with people. I think this town is a perfect place for the kind of makeovers I do." She set the plates on the table.

After she sat, he took a seat and he raised his glass of lemonade. "Here's to a prosperous business venture."

She clinked her glass against his and smiled like Mona Lisa. "And to a successful makeover. I mean, renovation."

Chapter Four

Nick was helping clear away the lunch dishes and wishing he could find an excuse to spend the rest of the afternoon at Maggie's place when the annoying sound of Allison's voice drifted down the hallway.

"Hello-o? Anyone home?"

The impromptu visit seemed to take Maggie by surprise. "Allison?" she called. "I'm in the kitchen."

"Does she come here often?" he asked quietly.

"No, and she always calls first. Maybe she wants to see you."

He couldn't tell if she was serious or not and didn't have time to ask before Allison sashayed into the room.

"Oh, Nick. This is a nice surprise."

Right. As if she hadn't noticed his truck parked in front of the house all morning. So why the pretense?

Maggie slid the plates onto a stack in the cupboard and closed the door. "Nick's been working on an estimate for renovations I need. He has some great ideas."

"That's nice. When do you start?"

Allison's attempt at small talk didn't fool Nick for a minute. "We're not sure." She definitely wanted something. Information?

"Where are the kids?" Maggie asked.

"John's taken the afternoon off and they've gone to the

children's zoo. He feels it's important that he spend quality time with them."

"That's so sweet." Maggie glanced at him. "Don't you think?"

"Yeah. Sweet."

"I received Leslie's wedding invitation yesterday," Allison said.

There it was—the motive for this unexpected visit. He leaned against the counter and crossed his arms. "Even I've been invited to witness the event, if you can imagine." And he now had one more reason not to go.

Maggie folded her dish towel and hung it up. "Leslie's your sister, right?"

He nodded, wondering how she knew that.

"When's the wedding?"

"Three weeks from Saturday."

Allison bestowed one of her smug glances on him. "She's asked me and Candice Bentley-Ferguson to be her bridesmaids. The subject of who you'll be taking to the wedding came up."

For once, he wished he wasn't always right about these things. First he had his mother hounding him, now Leslie and Allison. Didn't these women have anything better to do?

"Candice's divorce was finalized last week and I know for a fact that she doesn't have a date yet. You used to have a thing for Candice, as I recall."

Give me a break! That had been in the ninth grade. One make-out session at Billy Jean What's-her-name's birthday party was hardly "a thing."

Allison gave him a cool cat-that-stole-cream smile. "Candice said she'd go with you since you don't have a date."

How in hell did they know whether or not he had a date? "I hadn't wanted to rush things but I'd planned to ask Maggie to go with me."

Maggie's beautiful brown eyes popped open wide. "Me?"

"Why not? It'll give you a chance to…"

He stopped himself before he said, "wear those pearls." Their earlier conversation about the pearls had been fun, even a little flirtatious, and Allison's radar would detect that in a nanosecond. "It'll give you a chance to meet some of Collingwood Station's upper crust. Definitely a chance to improve your social standing." As soon as he said that, he wished he hadn't.

Allison gave him a steely glare.

"Thank you!" Maggie said. "I love weddings and I'd love to meet your family." Her quick acceptance was a little surprising, especially after his unnecessary remark about her social standing, but at least he was off the hook with Candice.

"Then it's settled."

He could tell Allison wasn't buying any of this and he felt as though he needed to do something to convince her that he'd really been planning to ask Maggie. So he moved closer to Maggie and casually draped an arm around her shoulders.

Big mistake.

It was one thing to go out of his way to provoke Allison but he didn't need to get this close to Maggie to do it.

Who knew she'd be the perfect height? Just tall enough that when they danced together at Leslie's wedding, her head would tuck nicely under his chin. She'd smell like strawberries and cream, and look up at him with those chocolatey eyes and when she spoke, that amazing voice would be for his ears only.

Definitely something to look forward to, but not a good idea to be thinking those things in front of Allison, who would be on the phone to his sister the minute she got home.

"I should go," he said. "I just need to run upstairs to check the attic for insulation. Do you have a stepladder?"

"I haven't seen one. I have a flashlight, if that'll help." She ducked out from under his arm and retrieved it from the cupboard under the sink.

"Thanks. I'll be right back." With any luck, Allison would be gone by then.

He took the stairs two at a time. The opening to the attic was in the hallway ceiling. He'd have to stand on something to reach it.

A kitchen chair?

No way was he going back downstairs. There had to be something upstairs.

Maggie's bedroom was to the right. The bed was neatly made but otherwise the room looked as though it'd been hit by a cyclone. Two suitcases, a stack of hat boxes and a couple of cardboard cartons took up most of the floor space. The top of an old dressing table was cluttered with hats and hairbrushes and jewelry, including the string of pearls.

He resisted the temptation to investigate further, except to see that the only chair in the room was an old wicker rocker heaped with clothes.

The two other bedrooms appeared to function as storage space and an office, judging by the books and papers strewn everywhere. He moved into the room to retrieve her office chair and couldn't resist taking a look at what she was working on. It stopped him dead in his tracks.

"I'll be damned." Then he grabbed the chair and headed out the door, grinning like a fool.

MAGGIE WOULD MUCH RATHER have gone upstairs with Nick than be in the kitchen, listening to Allison's chatter about Leslie's wedding and how it would be *the* event of the summer. She was relieved to finally hear Nick's footsteps on the stairs. When he walked into the kitchen to return the flashlight and say goodbye, his eyes held an odd combination of amusement and uncertainty.

"Gotta run," he said. "I'll drop off the estimate as soon as it's ready. Allison, it's been a pleasure, as always."

"You're leaving?" Allison seemed to forget all about the wedding. "I'll walk out with you. See you later, Maggie."

Maggie wondered if "later" meant the next time Nick was here.

He tucked his clipboard under his arm and headed out the front door, with Allison close behind. Less than a minute later, she heard his truck pull away. Apparently he didn't want to listen to Allison's chatter any more than she did.

Maggie was just glad they were gone. A jumble of emotions had her all aflutter and she needed time to sort them out.

Nick had asked her to be his date to his sister's wedding!

She knew better than to let the invitation send her spirits soaring, but she couldn't keep the bounce out of her step as she gathered her folders and sketches and sprinted up the stairs.

She felt like a teenager again, daydreaming about being asked to the prom by the coolest guy in school. Or the hottest, depending a person's perspective!

Yet, she needed to be realistic. Nick had invited her to the wedding so he could get out of taking someone named Candice and possibly to annoy Allison and his family. Not because he wanted to spend an evening with her. Besides, a man who was interested in a woman "that way" wouldn't give her a fruit basket. His gift had been funny and sweet, but about as far from romantic as a gift could get. And right after he'd asked her to the wedding—and she'd said yes—he'd suddenly been in a big hurry to leave.

Best not delude herself about Nick's intentions. Still, she'd learn a lot about him when she met his family. Nick Durrance deserved to be happy. Once he started working here, she'd have plenty of opportunities to help him find that happiness. She had a good feeling about that.

Until she reached the doorway of her office.

No!

She slammed the folders onto the bed.

No, no, no, no, no!

The yearbooks she'd been poring over last night were still lying on the floor. All of them open to the pages with Nick's pictures.

Had he come in here when he'd come up to check the insulation in the attic? He'd given her that odd look when he'd come downstairs. She'd thought it had something to do with Allison's endless talking, but what if…

Frantically she looked around for the access to the attic, relieved to see that it was in the hallway near the top of the stairs. He would have opened the hatch, looked inside and gone back downstairs. Nick didn't seem the type to snoop, and he would have had no reason to go any farther.

She returned to the office, gathered up the books and slipped the first one into place on the bookshelf.

How had he reached the access to the attic?

She went back into the hallway and took another look. He was tall but he wasn't *that* tall. He hadn't had a stepladder with him, which meant he must have stood on a chair.

Her desk chair.

Which meant he would have had to step right over the yearbooks to get it.

Oh, Maggie. You are such an airhead.

Everything that everyone had ever said about her was true. She rushed into things without thinking them through and she was flighty and impulsive. Of course, none of those things had anything to do with leaving the stupid yearbooks lying on the floor when she knew Nick was coming to inspect the house. That was beyond flighty. That was the dumbest thing she'd ever done.

Okay, so making a pair of wings out of an old patio umbrella and trying to fly off the roof of Aunt Margaret's garage had probably been the dumbest, but she'd only been eight years old. Now she was an adult.

What must Nick have thought when he'd seen his entire high-school history spread out on her office floor?

Oh, Maggie. You've really done it this time.

She cast a glance at the ceiling. "Aunt Margaret, I can't believe you let me do this. You always used to tell me to put my things away when I was finished with them. Why didn't you say something?"

She shoved the other three yearbooks onto the shelf.

Aunt Margaret's laughter filled the room.

"This is *not* funny." Ugh. Dead people had such a sick sense of humor.

Maggie looked around the room and tried to remember why she'd come up here, but all she could think about was what Nick might have been thinking.

"Darn. I really want to go to that wedding with him. What if he changes his mind?" But if she expected an answer, she'd have to wait for Aunt Margaret to stop laughing first.

As for Nick, she decided there was only one way to find out how he felt.

Ask him.

NICK SAT at the drafting table in his office, trying to focus on the floor plan and the list of materials he'd need, but concentrating on Maggie's renovations was difficult when all he could think about was Maggie.

Why on earth would she have been looking at those yearbooks? He tried to remember if he even owned copies. If he did, he hadn't seen them in years.

He definitely liked the idea that she'd been looking at them though. It meant she had more than a passing interest in him.

So?

So…he didn't know why that mattered but he still liked the idea. On the other hand, what if Allison had put her up to this? Was he really such a bad person that Allison Peters had to turn up and make his life miserable? Maybe he'd stored up a bunch of bad karma and now it was payback time.

Right. That sounded like something Maggie would say.

He knew how his family would react to him taking someone so unorthodox to the wedding. He indulged himself in a sly grin. *Yes, sirree.* For the first time in as long as he could remember, he was actually looking forward to a family function. But would Maggie survive a formal encounter with the Durrance family? She could always tell them their horoscopes, he thought with amusement. That alone would be worth the price of admission.

His conscience kicked him in the gut. Ticking off his family was not a good reason for asking a woman to go out with him. Especially Maggie.

He didn't know why but he couldn't stop thinking about her. *But the sooner you finish this estimate,* he reminded himself, *the sooner you'll get to see her again.*

He was busy punching numbers into his calculator when Brent Borden, his longtime friend and only employee, came in and tossed a roll of blueprints on the top of the filing cabinet. "Hey, boss. How's it going?"

"Good. I'm working up an estimate for Miss Meadowcroft's remodeling job."

"Sure hope we get that one. She sounds like a hot little number, from what everyone's saying."

"Yeah, well, she wants to turn her house into a spa, and there's a very good chance that Durrance Construction will get the job."

"All right! We can use the work, and here's hoping Miss Meadowcroft will be spending lots of time on the job with us."

Nick glared at him. "She lives there, so I think it's safe to say that she'll be around. And it'll help to remember that she's a client."

Brent's eyes went wide, then he burst out laughing. "I see," he drawled. "So that's how it's going to be."

"What's that supposed to mean?"

"Man, you have never given a damn if someone hustled a

pretty girl on the job site. I seem to recall that when we were hired to work at the massage parlor—"

Jeez. Nick should know by now that past mistakes always came back to bite him on the butt. "Maggie Meadowcroft isn't running a massage parlor. Her house is in a respectable neighborhood and she's a very nice woman—"

Brent was still laughing. "You sly dog. You've already put the moves on her!" He held up a hand and Nick reluctantly met his friend's high-five.

"Let me guess," Brent speculated. "A little pizza. A lot of beer. Wham, bam, thank you—"

"Hang on a minute. You got this all wrong." He might as well spill it, since Brent would hear about it sooner or later. "I haven't gone out with her. I just asked her to go to my sister's wedding."

Brent let out a long, low whistle. "You invited her to meet your family? Man. Either she's really special or you really have it in for her."

Nick sighed. "If I didn't have a date, Leslie and Allison were going to line me up with one."

Brent stopped laughing. "Allison?"

"Allison Peters," Nick said. "From high school. Remember?"

"Uh, yeah." Brent made a face that pretty much summed up Nick's feelings about that whole fiasco. "What about her?"

"She lives next door to Maggie, and she's my sister's bridesmaid and she just happened to drop by Maggie's this morning with the news that Candice Bentley-Ferguson is newly divorced and once again hot to trot. Oh, and did I mention, also one of my sister's bridesmaids? What was I supposed to do? Let myself get lassoed into taking her?"

"Quite the dilemma. Which you resolved by asking the new 'client' to go with you?"

Wiseass. It's not as though Brent had never gotten himself into a jam. "Okay," he agreed. "I wasn't thinking clearly. But you know my family. And Allison. What I was I supposed to do? Let them set me up with Candice?"

"Uh, no. You could have said, 'Gee, thanks for the offer, but I already have a date.' End of story."

Nick sighed again, heavier this time. "Yeah, well, I guess I wasn't thinking too clearly."

"No kidding." Brent put on that annoying squinty-eyed expression every time he thought deeply about something. "Unless you really wanted to ask Maggie all along."

Best to let that comment slide, Nick thought.

Brent seemed to have other ideas. "So? Did you want to?"

"Maybe." Although after the trouble with the masseuse, he should have learned his lesson. Never mix business with pleasure.

Brent grinned. A huge, oh-man-I-can't-believe-you-finally-fell-for-somebody grin. "This woman's really that special?"

"Sort of. No. I don't know." He thought about her zany hair and the rejuvenating face gunk. The crazy talk about ghosts and horoscopes. The makeover business. The yearbooks. Special wasn't exactly the right word. "I don't think so."

Brent rolled his eyes. "Very convincing."

Nick really wanted this conversation to end. "Since when did you become Mr. Analytical? I asked her to the wedding. She accepted. We're going. End of story. It'll be fine."

"Fine? Since when is it 'fine' to take a makeup artist to a Durrance family function?"

Nick sighed. "I don't know. Allison didn't like the idea. My family *really* won't like it, but what can I say? What's done is done."

"Freud would have had a field day with your family."

"Freud wouldn't have lasted five minutes with those women."

Chapter Five

Maggie was on the seventh trial of a new moisturizer when Nick dropped off his estimate. She'd spent all day concocting an explanation for the yearbook fiasco, which she'd intended to deliver the moment she saw him again. Problem was, she hadn't allowed for his arrival coinciding with her having a generous coating of peaches slathered all over her face.

Nick laughed and handed her an envelope. "Hard at work, I see."

Her timer buzzed. "Go on into the kitchen. It'll just take me a minute to wash this off."

She found him in the kitchen, sniffing the container of moisturizer.

"This stuff smells good enough to eat."

"Well, I wouldn't recommend it. It's the essential oils that make it smell so good but they're probably not the best thing to ingest. My strawberry facial mask is edible though. Quite delicious, actually."

He gave her an odd look. "Interesting."

She pulled a pencil out of her hair, scribbled a few notes in her coil-bound notebook and stabbed the pencil back in place. "I haven't quite worked out the right proportions for this one."

"Sounds pretty scientific." But he was grinning so broadly

that she couldn't tell if he was serious or if he was seriously making fun of her.

"Something funny?" She ran both hands over her face, thinking perhaps she'd missed some of the cream.

"You remind me of Wilma Flintstone."

"I hope you don't use that line very often. Most women don't like to imagine themselves as the cartoon wife of a pre-historic caveman."

He reached up and tucked a loose strand of hair behind the pencil. "You should be flattered. That was one of the best TV shows ever made."

Maggie wondered if Wilma had felt all wobbly and breath-less when Fred touched her hair. "It didn't seem very realistic."

"I don't know about that. Poor old Fred was really just a reg-ular guy trying to figure out how to make his wife happy."

"And did he? Figure it out?" she asked.

"No, and he's not alone. Women are complicated. Take Wilma's hair, for example. I always wondered why she had those bones sticking out of it."

"She wore her hair up, didn't she? I'm guessing the bones held it in place."

"I see. So not the same as using it as a place to store pencils?"

"Not the same thing at all. Pencil hair means a woman is working. Bone hair is strictly for effect."

"See? What did I tell you? Complicated."

She enjoyed the banter. "We're trained that way, you know, from birth. We have classes and everything."

He gave her a long, steady look that must have lasted a full fifteen seconds. "There isn't a man alive who would doubt that." Then the creases at the corners of his eyes deepened a little as he smiled. "I guess that's why we're always trying to perfect our game."

"It works both ways, you know. Women have a hard time un-derstanding men, too."

"What's to understand? Men are the simplest creatures alive. Feed them, flatter them and they're pretty much at your mercy."

"Is that what Wilma did for Fred?"

"Let's just say she had him figured out."

"I'll have to take your word for it."

"You never watched *The Flintstones?*"

She shook her head. "My parents thought television was the great corrupter of young minds, so we never had one."

"Really? That's…different."

Ha! He didn't know the half of it. From what Allison had told her about Nick's family, he'd grown up with all the material advantages that her parents had shunned. But while she'd been showered with affection, Nick had either been criticized or ignored. The urge to touch him, to reassure him that it was okay to be different, was overwhelming. But it was too soon for that.

"My childhood might have been different, but I wouldn't trade it for anything."

"Then you're very lucky."

"Yes, I am." She picked up her notebook and started to clear the table.

"What do you record in that lab manual of yours?"

"I keep track of the proportions of ingredients I use and make a note about the texture and feel of it. Eventually I find one or two that feel right, then I do more detailed tests."

"But no animal testing?"

She laughed at that. "No, but if I did, none of my products would be harmful to them. Everything I use is safe and natural. And organic."

"So how do you do a more detailed test?"

"I start experimenting. Today I'm working on a peaches-and-cream moisturizer. I'll try a few more variations, then narrow them down to the two or three I like best. Then I apply all three at once, to different parts of my face, and see how they feel. And Allison has been letting me use her as a guinea pig."

Mentioning Allison reminded her about the yearbooks. She really did have to say something about those and now would be as good a time as any. "Listen, about the other day—"

There was a knock at the front door, followed by Allison's characteristic "Hello-o?" Either this woman had really lousy timing, or she deliberately arranged her visits to coincide with the appearance of Nick's truck.

"This is really starting to get old," Nick said.

Maggie shrugged. "I haven't seen her since the last time you were here. Maybe it's you she wants to see."

She could hear Allison's footsteps cross the foyer. "Maggie? Are you home?"

"In the kitchen."

Allison wore a tailored shirt, a slim-fitting, knee-length skirt and a pair of sandals that were probably Italian and very expensive. Was this for Nick's benefit?

Whatever the reason for her glamorous neighbor's appearance, Maggie felt very badly put together. Her denim shorts and lavender T-shirt had become stained with peaches, thanks to a minor mishap with the food processor.

"Oh! Hello, Nick."

Oh, please, Maggie thought. *Why bother to pretend she hadn't known Nick was here?*

"I didn't expect to see you here. I came over to invite Maggie to our Fourth of July barbecue on Sunday. You will come, won't you?"

"Um, sure. Would you like me to bring something?"

"Just yourself. And Nick, of course." She directed a sugary smile at the man who had once been the love of her life, maybe even her first lover. The thought made Maggie uncomfortable, even though it was none of her business.

"You'll come to the party, too, won't you, Nick? John says he'd love to reconnect."

Nick didn't seem to buy that. "Sorry. I already have plans."

His refusal made Maggie regret her speedy acceptance.

"Oh, too bad," Allison said.

Maggie thought so, too. Going to the barbecue with Nick would have been fun. Kind of a casual predate before his sister's wedding. Unless, of course, the yearbook fiasco had made him change his mind about that.

Allison gave Maggie a conspiratorial wink. "It's just as well that Nick won't be there. Leslie and our friend Candice are coming and we'll have lots of time for girl talk." She actually giggled before she lowered her voice to a stage whisper. "We'll tell you all about when I dated Nick in high school."

Nick did not look amused. He looked as though his head might explode. "Did you mean *this* Sunday?"

"Of course. This Sunday is the Fourth of July."

"Just so happens that *this* Sunday I'm free. Looks like I can make it after all."

"Well, good. See you then." Allison glanced at the designer watch on her slender wrist. "Look at the time! I have a million things to do before the party, and John wants me to treat myself to a new outfit for Sunday night. Isn't that sweet?" She strode to the door as though Maggie's kitchen was the red carpet, then turned and struck a pose. "See you both on Sunday. Sixish?" she said before she breezed out of the room.

Maggie exchanged glances with Nick and for a minute they stood there, speechless.

"Did Fred and Wilma ever have a Fourth of July barbecue?" she asked.

Nick's laughter broke the tension. "Are you sure you never saw that show?"

"Positive. And about the party. I hope you didn't agree to go on my account. I would have been fine on my own."

"You think she wasn't serious about filling your head with wild stories about my past?"

"I'm pretty sure she wasn't serious." Besides, her head wasn't like a sponge that soaked up every tidbit of gossip that came along. She'd listen carefully to anything she heard about Nick, but she wouldn't necessarily believe it.

"Trust me. When it comes to telling tales out of school, she's dead serious."

"Well, I'm not in the habit of believing everything I hear. And, um, while we're on the subject of school…" She took a deep breath and plunged in. "I have a confession to make." She could tell from the way he looked at her that he already knew what she was going to say.

"Remember the other day when you went upstairs to check the insulation in the attic? You probably noticed that I'd been looking at Aunt Margaret's old yearbooks from your high school."

She tried to read his expression, but he wasn't giving anything away. "Yeah," he said. "I noticed. Please tell me that Allison didn't put you up to it."

Although it was tempting to let him think that, it wasn't the truth. "As far as I know, Allison doesn't even know the yearbooks are here. But she'd said…she said that when you were in high school, you broke the heart of every woman…girl…who tried to refor—" *Watch what you say, Maggie.* "Every girl you dated. I was curious."

Nick's eyes narrowed. "There are two sides to every story, you know. And the world would be a lot better off if people like Allison would mind their own business."

Maggie tried her best to be diplomatic. "I think she was trying to warn me that if you…if you and I…"

Nick was staring at her.

Way to go, Maggie. Talk about an utter lack of finesse.

"Exactly what did she say?" he finally asked.

"Nothing! Really, this was my fault. Allison said you broke a lot of hearts and I guess I just wanted to see for myself."

Nick crossed his arms over his chest. "And?"

An uncomfortable heat started to creep up her neck. "And what?"

"What did you find out?"

"About what?"

"About me being a heartbreaker."

How was she supposed to answer that question? *You were, and still are.*

Nick grinned at her. "Was that a yes?"

"What makes you think that?"

"You nodded your head. That usually means yes."

Her face was completely on fire at that point and to make matters worse, Aunt Margaret was having a good laugh. Well, they weren't getting the best of her. Not over something as silly as this. "If you have a history of breaking hearts, I'll have to take everyone's word for it. I have no experience with that sort of thing."

"You've never had your heart broken?"

Only by two men who never knew how she felt about them, so that didn't count. She glanced down at the floor. "No. Never."

He hooked a finger under her chin and forced her to look at him. "Then that means Maggie Meadowcroft is one of the lucky ones."

His hand was warm and a little rough, and at that precise moment, she felt luckier than she had ever felt. "I guess it does." Except that she'd always thought she would have risked everything, even a broken heart, to have had the attention of a guy like Nick.

He let her go and abruptly stepped back. "I think we'd better go over this estimate. As soon as we decide where and when to start, I'll order the materials."

An hour later they'd moved past the awkwardness and decided tearing out the wall and renovating the bathroom would be the best place to start because that work would take the longest.

"We can get to work first thing Monday morning but I'll stop by on Sunday, just before six, so we can go to the barbecue together."

"You don't have to pick me up. I'll be fine on my own."

He gave her a lopsided smile. "I was kind of hoping *I* wouldn't have to go alone."

Was he really that insecure about being with old friends? If that was the case, he really did need her help. "No problem," she said. "I'll be happy to go with you."

AT FIVE MINUTES to six on Sunday, Nick turned onto Maggie's block and slowed almost to a stop. Both sides of the street were lined with cars, which could only mean one thing. Allison's "little" barbecue was anything but.

Great, he thought. Why had he agreed to this? He glanced at Maggie's front door. There was one good reason. He had a date, sort of, and he needed to do damage control before his old high-school flame filled Maggie's head with a load of crap.

Why did women have to make things so complicated? It had been a good while since he'd met a woman who interested him as much as Maggie did, and he'd never met one who seemed so remarkably uncomplicated. A little off-the-wall, maybe. Even a little spooky with her ability to know what he was thinking, but not complicated. Or clingy and controlling. Or any of the things that drove him nuts about the women in his family. Maggie was happy and secure and self-confident. Yes, this was definitely a first for him.

And he was pretty sure the feeling was mutual, if her checking out his old high-school photos was anything to go on. Not to mention the whole heartbreaker thing. He didn't believe she was inexperienced enough to have never had her heart broken but even if that were true, he'd wager she'd broken a few herself. Unintentionally, maybe, but broken them just the same.

That she was his client made him a little uneasy, but it wasn't as if they were going to end up in bed or anything. He'd bet she didn't move that fast and, for once, that was fine with him.

He reached for the box on the seat next to him, had second thoughts and pulled his hand back, then grabbed it and jumped out of his truck. He'd already knocked on the door when he was hit by the second wave of second thoughts.

"Hi."

Too late. "Hi. Wow. You look amazing."

And that was an understatement. She had on a denim mini-skirt that showed a generous length of leg, thank you very much, and a purple tank top that hinted at cleavage without actually revealing any. The men at the party wouldn't mind, since they'd get to spend the evening admiring those legs, and Nick didn't mind, since he didn't want to spend the evening watching other men gawking down the front of her shirt.

"Thank you. You look pretty good yourself, although I expected you to be a little more casual."

Nick had toyed with the idea but instead of giving the high-society tongue-waggers any more to talk about than they already had, he'd done his best to look like part of the country-club set. Seeing Maggie in casual clothes made him wish he hadn't bothered to press his khaki Hilfiger's and buy a new golf shirt. It wasn't as though he ever went golfing. He shouldn't worry about what other people thought. Maggie didn't. And when people got an eyeful of that saucy little skirt, they'd have something to say.

"Everything else was in the laundry," he said.

"I hate it when that happens. I just have to grab my plate and I'll be ready to go."

She seemed to float down the hallway in a pair of sandals that were tied on with crisscrossed ankle straps. Oh, yeah. People would talk. No question.

A minute later she reappeared with a huge tray piled with cookies. Be interesting to see Allison's reaction to that.

"I made these," she said. "What are you taking?"

"Where?"

"To the barbecue. In the box you're carrying."

"Oh, right. It's not for the barbecue, it's for you."

"For me? Another present?"

"Not really. No. It's not a present. It's for the construction project. Here, open it." For some reason his brain was only sending intermittent signals to his tongue.

He held the plate and watched her set the box on the hall table and lift the lid.

"A scrapbook? What's it for?"

"Well, I remembered how you had all those sketches and color samples in a folder and I thought you might like to keep a record of the renovations. Photos, that sort of thing. But if it's too corny—" He waited for her reaction.

"I love it! It's a great idea. We can do lots of before-and-after pictures and paste in scraps of the old wallpaper and curtains and…" She grinned widely. "We can put it on display when the spa opens. We'll call it 'the story of a makeover.' Customers will love it. Thank you."

He liked that she said "we" instead of "I," even though he didn't have the guts to tell that this makeover business would never fly. He was also relieved she didn't think he was being too forward by bringing her another gift. Choosing gifts for women had always been damned difficult, but Maggie was different. Lately he kept noticing things he'd never paid attention to before and wondering what she would think of them.

"Are you ready to go? These cookies smell great, by the way. What'd you put in them?"

She gave him a sly wink. "My secret ingredient. It makes them irresistible."

"I hope it's legal."

She laughed. "In all fifty states."

"Let's go then." Allison's Fourth of July barbecue was almost certain to be a catered affair and he could hardly wait to see her reaction to Maggie's irresistible, and obviously homemade, cookies.

Chapter Six

Nick hadn't realized just how insecure he felt about facing these people until his hand was on the gate. Although he'd lived in Collingwood Station all his life, he rarely saw the people he went to school with. It always amazed him how easy it was to avoid the champagne and caviar set when you lowered your standards to pizza and beer. Except it didn't feel lower. He'd take a cold beer over a two-hundred-and-fifty-dollar bottle of bubbly any day.

She smiled up and leaned into him a little. "Wow. I wasn't expecting this."

He put a hand on her shoulder. Unfortunately this was exactly what he'd expected.

The fence had been liberally draped with red, white and blue bunting. A bar, complete with a tuxedoed bartender, had taken up residence on the deck and beneath a huge blue-and-white-striped tent, a chef in a tall white hat was fussing over the tables loaded with food.

"Everything looks perfect," Maggie said.

Perfectly extravagant.

Right down to the hostess who was strolling across the lawn toward them. Allison had attired herself in a strapless sundress and a pair of elegant flat-soled shoes that were probably Prada, or something equally expensive. "I'm so glad you could make it. Happy Fourth of July! Welcome to our little gathering."

"Little" being a relative term in Allison's vocabulary. There had to be forty or fifty people at this shindig and Nick swore every single one of them had stopped what they were doing and were now staring at him and Maggie.

"What's this?" Allison asked when she spied the plate in Maggie's hands.

"Cookies," Maggie said. "They're homemade."

"Oh. How…thoughtful. Thank you."

"I thought the kids would like them."

Allison looked puzzled. "The children are spending the weekend with my parents. You really didn't have to go to all this trouble."

"It was no trouble."

Nick loved that she was genuinely unaware of their host's discomfort.

Allison looked at him, as though for support. What? She thought he should tell Maggie to take the cookies back to her place? Not a chance.

"Why don't you help yourself to drinks while I give these to André?" She glared at Nick, then strode away.

He watched her carry Maggie's offering across the lawn. As she stepped under the tent, she glanced back at them. He smiled at her and nodded. She'd been checking to see if they were watching. If they hadn't been, Maggie's "irresistible" cookies would have done a disappearing act.

The chef looked just as surprised as Allison had when she presented Maggie's contribution to the festivities. Even from across the yard, Nick could see the man's eyebrows knit together as he shook his head. Once again Allison glanced their way and briefly met Nick's gaze. Then she pulled herself up to her full height and shoved the plate toward the white-suited chef. The man threw up his hands in a dramatic gesture, snatched it from her and carried it over to the dessert table.

To Nick's relief, Maggie was admiring the crowd and the decorations like a child who'd just seen her first snowfall. Come to think of it, a nice blizzard would certainly put an end to this nightmare.

"Do you know all these people?" Maggie asked.

Another quick glance around. "Let's say we're acquainted. And I'd say that calls for a drink."

Two uniformed waiters strolled through the crowd, one with hors d'oeuvres and another with a tray of crystal flutes.

"Would you like a glass of champagne?" he asked.

She wrinkled her nose. "No thanks. Champagne doesn't seem like the right thing for a barbecue."

No kidding. "Come on, then. We'll grab something at the bar."

Bad decision. John Fontaine, Allison's husband, stood near the bar, talking to Candice, and it was too late to distract Maggie. She had already stepped onto the deck and was heading straight into the fray.

"Nick!" John's handshake was limp and a little too sweaty for Nick's liking. "Good to see you, buddy. How long has it been?"

Buddy? Yeah, right. John had gone off to college and stolen his girlfriend, which meant he'd actually done Nick a favor, but that hardly made them buddies.

"You remember Candice, don't you?"

The woman forced herself into his arms, presenting one cheek, then the other. Nick had no choice but to kiss both of them. She reeked of sex and expensive perfume.

She ran her hands down his chest. "So this is what hard labor does for a man's body. You know, I need to have a few repairs done. Maybe you can bring your tools over to my place sometime." She gave John a sly wink as she said it.

Nick's skin crawled as he held her by the wrists and backed away before letting her go. He hastily draped an arm around

Maggie's shoulders. Using her to deflect Candice's come-on was a bad idea but he couldn't think fast enough to come up with an alternative, and he really hoped Maggie recognized it as signal to go along with him.

Maggie responded by leaning close and resting her head against his shoulder. Man, he really owed her for this.

"Maggie's keeping me pretty busy," he said, giving her shoulder a gentle squeeze. "Have you met Maggie Meadowcroft?"

Candice's gaze slid in Maggie's direction. "Oh, hello." She took in Maggie's casual attire and seemed ready to dismiss her. "Did you say Meadowcroft? That sounds familiar."

If Maggie picked up on the woman's hostility, she didn't let on. "Margaret Meadowcroft was my great-aunt. She used to teach English at Collingwood High School."

Candice laughed. "Of course! Oh, I haven't thought of Miss Meadowcroft in years!"

Nick figured she hadn't thought of anyone but herself in years.

"Wasn't she the teacher who gave you all those detentions, Nick? I seem to recall—"

"That was a long time ago, Candice. Why don't you tell us what you've been up to since high school? I hear you just got divorced. And I always thought you and Mark were a match made in heaven."

The woman's insincere laughter bugged the hell out of him. "Silly you," she said. "Mark and I only lasted a little over a year. Come to think of it, our divorce took longer than that. I've been married and divorced twice since then."

"I see." Which he didn't. Although all that wedded bliss probably explained the wealth of diamonds she was flashing around. Divorce must be profitable.

"Thank God for Allison and John. Allie's been my rock through all this. And John..." She snuggled intimately against her best friend's husband's shoulder. "John has handled my last two divorces."

The tension between John and Candice was strung as tight as a banjo and if Nick had to guess, he'd say that John had handled a lot more than her litigation.

What was it with these people? They turned personal relationships into a blood sport. Nick would be the first to admit he was no saint and that's why he wasn't married. He tried to look John in the eye but the man was suddenly intent on something on the other side of the yard. Nick followed his gaze.

Allison.

No doubt John hoped his wife hadn't witnessed that last little exchange. Lucky for him, Allison was too busy being the perfect hostess.

Nick still had his arm around Maggie and he took advantage of it to steer her toward the bar. "How 'bout we get that drink? Will you excuse us?" he said to John and Candice.

"That was awkward," he said as soon as they were out of earshot.

"I'll say. Three marriages," Maggie whispered. "Wow. That's…" She actually seemed to be at a loss for words, which had to be a rare occasion for Maggie Meadowcroft.

Nick helped her out. "Insane?" he suggested. "Obscenely ridiculous?"

Amusement lit up her eyes. "So, are you going to take her up on the offer to use your tools?"

"Excuse me?"

"She asked you to do some carpentry work for her. That is what she wanted, isn't it?" But her innocent look didn't fool him for a minute.

"You have a wicked streak, Miss Meadowcroft."

She grinned. "You don't know the half of it."

He glanced back over his shoulder in time to see Allison crossing the lawn to join John and Candice. He dipped his head toward Maggie's ear and lowered his voice. "You'd think he'd cool it with the mistress while his wife's around."

Maggie looked startled. "Is that what you think is going on? I didn't get that sense, at all. I mean, don't get me wrong. Candice wouldn't give it a second thought, but John is going along with her because she's a client. What do business people call it? Schmoozing?"

"Do you always find a way to see the best in people?"

"I see all kinds of things in people. I'm sure you're wrong about John but—" she lowered her voice some more "—whatever you're thinking about Candice is probably bang on."

Far be it from him to dispute a woman's intuition.

The bartender handed two glasses of wine to the couple ahead of them and wiped the counter. "What would you like, madam?"

Maggie leaned across the counter. "What do you have that's cold and nonalcoholic?" She grinned up at Nick. "Alcohol goes straight to my head. I guess you could say I'm a cheap drunk."

Nick couldn't say why, exactly, but he filed that information away for future reference.

"Mineral water? Iced tea with lemon?" the bartender suggested.

"Oooh, iced tea, please."

"Excellent choice, ma'am And you, sir?"

"I'll have a beer."

"Of course, sir."

They picked up their drinks, turned from the bar and ran straight into his sister.

"Nick? This is a surprise." Leslie wasn't looking at him though. She was studying Maggie like a court transcript. "How are you?"

Damn. He'd hoped to avoid family entanglements until the day of the wedding but he should have known he couldn't avoid Leslie. Maybe he could at least avoid getting into a dull conversation with Gerald Bedford III.

"Good. How are you?"

"I'm well, thank you."

"And Mother?"

Leslie forced a smile. "She's fine. Busy with wedding arrangements."

Now that he knew everyone was well and fine, he wasn't sure what else to say.

Leslie, on the other hand, was never at a loss for words. "Are you going to introduce me to your friend?"

"Yes. Sorry. Leslie, this is Maggie Meadowcroft. She lives next door in her aunt's…"

"I know who she is, silly. Allison's told me all about the two of you."

That figured. "I'm renovating Maggie's house."

"And bringing her to the wedding. And to neighborhood gatherings, I see." Leslie gave him a patronizing smile. "Mother's been hoping you'd call. She was disappointed that she had to hear about Maggie from someone else."

The remark was laced with innuendo and completely uncalled for. What was there to hear? "I'm renovating Maggie's house," he repeated. "I've been meaning to call but I've been busy." They both knew it was a lie, but in his family, telling a lie was acceptable as long as it didn't make the person you were lying to look bad.

"I can imagine you've been very busy." Leslie shifted her attention away from Nick and let it settle on Maggie, this time more like a real-estate appraiser looking at a fixer-upper. Finally she extended a hand.

Maggie ignored the offer of a handshake and gave his sister an enthusiastic hug instead. "I love weddings and I'm so glad we've had a chance to meet before yours. You're going to make a beautiful bride. Isn't she, Nick?"

Nick's family liked to avoid physical contact whenever possible and he could see that the hug had robbed Leslie of some of her composure. Although he wasn't sure what Maggie was up to, he decided to play along. "It'll be difficult to improve on perfection, but yes, she'll be more beautiful than ever."

For the first time in as long as Nick could remember, Leslie seemed to have nothing to say. And she was blushing. The heightened color suited her, making her look younger and more relaxed than she had in ages. For the first time in his life, or hers, she was looking at him with what he would swear was something that approached genuine affection.

"What a lovely thing to say. Thank you." Then she turned to Maggie. "I'm so glad you're coming to the wedding with Nick. It was nice to meet you. I have to get back to Gerald—my fiancé—and it looks as though we're ready to eat, but I hope we have a chance to talk some more before the party's over."

"Me, too," Maggie said.

As soon as Leslie was out of earshot, Nick looked down at his companion. "Thank you."

"For what?"

"I'm not sure, but I can't remember the last time I had a conversation with a member of my family that didn't end with me getting a lecture about what I need to do to improve my life." And not in a million years had he expected his sister to say that she was pleased he was taking someone from outside the Durrance family's social circle to her wedding.

Maggie broadsided him with that bewitching smile of hers. "Maybe she misses having a big brother in her life."

Nick doubted that, but just the same he looked around the crowd and wondered how many more surprises were in store for him tonight.

MAGGIE ADMIRED the long buffet table that had been set up under the tent. She had never seen so much food in one place and everything looked delicious. She filled her plate with small amounts of various salads, being careful to leave room for whatever the chef was carving at the far end of the table.

"I want to try a little of everything but I don't think my plate is big enough," she said.

Nick was right behind her, filling his own plate. "There's a lot of food here, all right."

"I'll say. I was expecting hot dogs and corn on the cob," she said. "Maybe hamburgers."

"At a Collingwood Station Fourth of July barbecue? Thrown by Allison Peters Fontaine? What made you think that?"

"Allison has kids, so I assumed this would be a family party." After all, wasn't that what holidays were all about? Family? But there wasn't a child in sight, which was why Allison had been so surprised by the cookies. Maggie had also assumed the party would be potluck. Aside from two weddings and a friend's bar mitzvah years ago, she had never been to a catered party.

Nick leaned close and spoke into her ear. "You have a lot to learn about high society. But here's your corn on the cob."

She laughed. The cobs had been sliced into small chunks and lightly grilled. She selected one and added it to the growing pile on her plate. "I'm afraid I won't be able to eat all of this."

"No problem. One of the advantages of Collingwood Station high society is that no one worries about the starving children in the rest of the world. Take as much as you want and throw away what you can't eat."

"Ouch. Don't be too hard on these people, Nick. They're your friends and family."

"Yeah, well, don't you be too easy on them. They'll eat you alive."

Nick's comment reminded her of how much work she had ahead of her. She didn't look at life the way he did, always suspecting that people had an ulterior motive for everything they did. When people knew she believed the best about them, they usually lived up to her expectations. Nick would catch on eventually.

But he also had a kind of vulnerability that brought out a woman's protective instincts and made her want to let go of all reason, settle into those arms of his and reassure him that everything would be all right.

Well, Maggie Meadowcroft had a big heart, but it belonged to her. She looked up and caught his smile. Who was she kidding? She'd definitely sample those arms if they were offered, but she'd hang on to her heart.

THE LAWN WAS DOTTED with white cloth-covered tables set for six. Candice waved to them from across the yard but Maggie appeared not to see her and Nick did his best to ignore her, too. He followed Maggie to an unoccupied table and while he hated to think who might join them, at least it wouldn't be Candice. He hoped.

Maggie unrolled her napkin and laid the cutlery on either side of her plate before carefully spreading the napkin over her thighs. The short denim skirt revealed a lot of leg and it seemed a shame to cover it.

Within a few minutes they were joined by two couples he didn't recognize until they introduced themselves.

Simon and Jocelyn Cartwright and Martin and Francine Thompson. Jocelyn was a contemporary of his sister's and Simon had been the student council president in Nick's senior year. He hadn't thought about high school in years but this week it had come back to haunt him with a vengeance.

Simon was the CEO of a large electronics firm in the city. Jocelyn owned a small, exclusive dress shop in Collingwood Station. Martin had his own engineering firm and Francine was a lawyer. She and Allison's husband worked at the same law firm.

Nick hadn't thought of it before now but he assumed Maggie

had gone to college. Which made him the only person at the table who didn't have a college degree. Instead he ran a sometimes-successful construction company and spent his free time playing pool and drinking beer with other tradespeople. Most of them hadn't even finished high school, which usually made him feel pretty well-educated.

Whatever Maggie's background was, she seemed blissfully unimpressed by Collingwood Station's uppercrust and chatted openly and unselfconsciously with their dinner companions. "This is such a wonderful garden," she said as she helped herself to a dinner roll and passed the basket to Martin. "I love that the old homes in this neighborhood have such big backyards and all these enormous oak trees."

"Are you the person who's renovating the old house next door?" Jocelyn asked.

"Yes. Nick's company is doing the work for me."

Nick caught their exchange of knowing glances. Bad enough that they speculated about his private life. He hated to think they'd start to gossip about Maggie. Especially since there was nothing to gossip about, and he was going to make sure it stayed that way.

"It's a big house for one person," Francine said.

"My aunt managed," Maggie reminded her. "I like to think the Meadowcroft women are capable of anything."

No one seemed to have a response, and Nick knew the feeling. She often left him speechless and he'd only known her for a few days.

"Besides, I'm turning the main floor into a day spa, so I won't actually be living in the whole house."

Jocelyn, who had been carefully slicing corn kernels off the cob, laid her knife and fork on her plate and both she and Francine leaned forward eagerly.

"A spa?" they chorused.

"What a great idea! Collingwood Station has never had one."

Jocelyn waved a manicured hand at her friend. "Francine's right. We've always had to go into the city."

Oh, the hardship.

Maggie took two purple and gold cards out the pocket of her skirt and passed them across the table. "Not anymore. Maggie Meadowcroft, makeover specialist. At your service."

"Inner Beauty?" Francine asked.

"What a great name," Jocelyn said. "When do you plan to open?"

The whole exchange was more than a little surprising. Either Maggie's cards didn't say anything about her food-based makeovers, or being pampered was so important that these two were willing to overlook the yogurt and Cream of Wheat.

"We'll work as fast as we can," he said, "but it'll take at least three weeks to get the place ready for business."

"While that's going on, there won't be a whole lot I can do in the house," Maggie said. "It'll be a perfect time for me to work in my garden." She picked up her grilled corn and chomp-chomp-chomped around the cob. "Mmm, delicious. Too bad it isn't the whole cob."

"These large properties are a lot of work," Martin said. "But well worth the effort."

"Yes, definitely worth it. We use the same gardener as Allison," Francine said. "I'm sure Allie will give you his number."

Which told them how much work Martin actually did on his "large property."

"Oh, I plan to do my own yard work. I love gardening and so did my aunt Margaret, although she wasn't able to do much of it as she got older."

"Martin also knows an excellent landscape architect," Francine said. "Don't you, darling? Maybe you can give Maggie a referral. I'm sure he can give you lots of great design ideas."

Maggie's eyes widened. "I don't think gardens are meant to

be planned. They should be wild and natural and unrestrained. I'll just feel my way through it. The garden will tell me what it wants to be."

Nick choked back a laugh as their four dinner companions were rendered speechless, again.

Maggie seemed unaware of the reaction she'd just generated. "Look at this yard, for example. The fence over there by the gate would be a beautiful backdrop for taller plants. Delphiniums, maybe. And that back corner would be a perfect place for a play area for the children. If I had kids and this was my yard, I'd build a tree house in that big old oak."

Jocelyn agreed about the flowers. "Hardly anyone plants delphiniums anymore, but you're right, they'd make a lovely contrast against the white fence."

"I'm not sure about the tree house though," Francine said. "I'd worry about being sued if one of my children's friends fell out and hurt themselves."

Nick wasn't sure what delphiniums were, but he agreed with the tree house idea. No one who saw this backyard would ever guess that two children lived here. His parents' house had been the same. The house and yard were impressive, but not places for living.

Maggie's children would have a place to run and play and have make-believe adventures in a tree house nestled in the arms of a big old oak. Her husband would be able to put his feet up on the coffee table and at night, he'd have his own pair of arms to settle into. He imagined that sleeping with Maggie would be another kind of adventure.

Whoa! That sounded awfully domestic for a man everyone knew couldn't be domesticated.

Jocelyn got up from the table. "Anyone for dessert?"

Francine stood and joined her. "Why not? I'll have to do an extra hour at the gym this week, but it'll be so worth it."

"You men just sit here and relax," Jocelyn said. "We'll surprise you." Then she glanced at Maggie. "Join us?" she asked, almost as an afterthought. "It'll give these men a chance for some guy talk."

"Sure. Thanks."

Martin refilled his wineglass and Simon's. "Care for some?" he asked Nick.

Nick shook his head.

"How's the construction business these days?" Simon asked.

Nick wondered why he'd care. "It keeps me busy."

"I've heard a lot of good things about your work. Jocelyn's been talking about expanding her shop. Would you be willing to take a look at it?"

Nick was on the verge of saying no. He made a point of not doing business with family and old high-school acquaintances who thought they were better than he was. But he found himself wondering what Maggie would say.

Go for it, is what she'd tell him.

"I'll be busy with Maggie's place for the next few weeks but if it can wait till after that, I'll be happy to take a look at it."

"No hurry. Give me a call when you're finished and we'll set something up."

"Sure thing."

Then Simon asked Martin if they were still on for golf on Wednesday afternoon and Martin asked Simon if he'd had a chance to call the investment broker he'd recommended. Since Nick didn't golf and had invested what little capital he had in his business, he leaned back in his chair and watched the women over at the dessert table.

From a distance, Maggie's purple tank top and short denim skirt looked even more out of place next to the casual designer clothes of the other women, but she talked and laughed with them as though they were old friends.

She sure was something. Other women worked at being attractive and sexy. Maggie didn't have to try, she just had it. He couldn't even say what "it" was, but he recognized it when he saw it. Judging by the way she turned the head of every male in the place, they saw it, too.

Nick let his chest puff out a little. Although this wasn't a date, they'd come to the party together and most people seemed to assume they were a couple. With a lot of women, he'd have been quick to point out that wasn't the case but he liked that everyone believed Maggie saw something in him that made him a worthwhile companion.

Her self-confidence rubbed off on him and he liked that, too. Come to think of it, he no longer completely dreaded his sister's wedding.

MAGGIE THOUGHT the dessert table looked even more tempting than the dinner buffet. The red-white-and-blue color scheme had been carried over to the New York cheesecakes that were decorated with fresh strawberries and blueberries. Her cookies had almost disappeared but she took one and put it on the plate for Nick. She piled on an array of other goodies and turned to find Jocelyn and Francine waiting for her. They each held two sparsely covered plates and were eyeing the single plate that she had loaded with goodies.

"Nick loves dessert," she said, hoping that was true. "And we always share," she added mischievously.

All evening she'd been able to tell that these women were speculating about her relationship with Nick. Might as well give them a little more to talk about. They had homes and families and well-established careers, but if they really had it all, why concern themselves with an old high-school friend who'd chosen a different path?

Unless they were a little envious. Or a lot envious.

Most of these men were Nick's age and they all had wives,

kids, mortgages and high-pressure jobs. Nick had none of those things, except the job, and she knew he loved what he did. He'd told her he lived in an apartment, which meant no mortgage. Allison would have told her if he'd ever had a wife and kids.

Maggie had no trouble imagining why these women were so interested in Nick. He was everything they didn't want in a husband, but everything they wanted in a man.

And you'd do well to remember that, she told herself.

Nick Durrance was not the marrying kind. Anyone could see that. Neither was she, but that didn't mean a girl couldn't have a little fun.

She set the plate of desserts on the table in front of him and caught his appreciative smile. She leaned close and whispered into his ear, "I got a little carried away and I had to tell Jocelyn and Francine that you love dessert. Please don't make a liar out of me."

He caught her hand in his and moved it to his lips. "My favorite dessert of all," he said. Then he eyed the contents of the plate. "I like all this stuff, too."

Maggie sat before her knees buckled but she never took her eyes off Nick.

He picked up the cookie and looked at her again while he took a bite. "I've been looking forward to this all night."

The back of her hand still tingled from the firm touch of his lips and the rough stubble on his chin. Who would have guessed it would feel so sexy? So instead of behaving, she threw caution to the wind and decided to keep on flirting with him. Except it no longer felt as though it was for the benefit of their dinner companions.

"What do you think of my cookies?" she asked.

Nick's eyes went dark. "I think we should wait till we're alone before I answer that."

Chapter Seven

Two hours later Nick was still waiting for an opportunity to answer Maggie's question. But she'd insisted they stay for the fireworks that John set off at the far end of the yard, which had turned out to be more fun than he'd expected. Especially since most of his enjoyment came from watching Maggie's wide-eyed delight.

"I adore fireworks," she'd said after John launched the last Roman candle. "It's too bad Allison's kids couldn't have been here."

"That's true," he said, although he couldn't muster much sympathy for two little kids he'd never met. Especially not when he had much more grown-up things on his mind. "It's getting late. Let me walk you home?"

He half expected her to say it wouldn't be necessary but instead she smiled up at him. "That would be nice. We should say good-night to Allison and John before we leave."

John was nowhere to be seen but they found Allison sitting at a table with Leslie.

"Thank you for such a great party," Maggie said, giving their hostess a friendly hug. "I had a wonderful time." Then she turned to Leslie and hugged her, too. "And I'm so pleased we had a chance to meet. I'm really looking forward to your wedding."

This time the hug didn't catch Leslie off guard and the smile she gave Maggie was genuinely friendly. "I'm glad you'll be there. You've done wonders with my big brother."

That was an odd thing for her to say, Nick thought. It wasn't as if he and Maggie were dating, and she was trying to make him into something he wasn't. They hardly knew each other, but he could spot meddlers a mile away and Maggie wasn't one of them.

"Please say good-night to John for me. And Gerald."

"Of course," Allison said. "He's tidying up the stuff from the fireworks."

"I'm not sure where Gerald is," Leslie said. She took a quick look around the yard. "I haven't seen him in a while."

"Maybe he's helping John," Maggie said. "Anyway, tell them both we said good-night."

Nick really didn't care where they were, he just wanted to get going. "Ready?" he asked.

Maggie nodded. "I sure am." And if those smiling eyes were sending him a message, it was too dark to read it. But a guy could hope, couldn't he?

Allison was watching them with open interest. "I hope you're glad you joined us tonight, Nick."

"I am. Thanks for inviting me. Us. It's been great."

And he meant it. The night had been full of surprises. Simon had invited him to play tennis on Wednesday. Martin asked him to drop by and take a look at his garage roof, which seemed to be leaking and then there was Jocelyn's store renovation. Leslie had taken him aside to talk about her wedding and she'd asked him if he would walk her down the aisle. He was damned sure their mother would not be happy about it, but he accepted.

It had been an amazing evening, and it wasn't over. He was about to take Maggie home and tell her what he thought about her cookies.

She looped her arm through his and they strolled across the

backyard toward the gate, saying good-night to several people along the way. It surprised him that he felt so good about this. Confident. All these years he'd been so sure these people were looking down their noses at him. Turns out they hadn't been thinking about him at all. And now that he'd reappeared, they seemed to accept him as he was.

He was about to open the gate for Maggie when she stopped. "I forgot my plate. I'll be right back." She dashed back to the serving tent.

Nick stepped into the shadows near the corner of the house and watched the crowd until a movement at the back door caught his attention. Gerald seemed to be doing his best to sneak out of the house, and he might have been successful if he hadn't had so much to drink. Then Candice Bentley-Ferguson appeared right behind him, giggling and trying to straighten her mussed-up hair.

What the hell?

The two of them went their separate ways across the yard and Nick tried to convince himself that what he'd just seen was probably nothing. But what if it wasn't?

He watched Gerald approach the table where Leslie was sitting. She glanced up with a smile, and he leaned down and dropped a casual kiss on the top of her head.

Okay. That was good. That meant he'd likely misinterpreted what he'd just seen.

Right?

Absolutely. Because if he believed that Gerald and Candice were messing around, then he'd be obligated to say something to Leslie. But Nick Durrance had a strict do-not-meddle policy and he'd really, really hate to have to deviate from it.

Maggie reappeared with her cookie plate tucked into the crook of her elbow. "Ready to go?"

He offered his arm. "Ready if you are."

She linked her arm with his. "I'm ready."

Since she only had to walk twenty yards, he couldn't say why he felt the need to escort her to her front door.

It was obvious he wanted to kiss her. For that, he needed to get her away from Allison and Leslie and all those other curious eyes before he dared try.

Why? He'd never worried about anything like that before. If he wanted to kiss a woman, he kissed her. And he had a damned good track record. Not once, ever, had he been rebuffed.

Maggie was different. She was sweet and funny and totally unpredictable. If he made a move that took her by surprise, she'd be just as likely to let him have it as let him have his way.

Also, there were his old friends, who seemed to have some newfound respect for him. He couldn't say exactly why it was important, but he didn't want to screw that up.

And then he and Maggie were standing on her front steps and he wasn't sure that kissing her was such a good idea, anyway.

Starting tomorrow, he'd be here every day, working for her. But right now those dark brown eyes were holding him hostage and tomorrow seemed a very long time away.

Maggie turned to face him, her back to the door.

He moved closer and she stood her ground.

He was way overthinking this. "I want to kiss you," he said.

She ran her hands along his arms. "I'd like that."

"Really?"

"Yes, really."

"You want to know something?"

"What?"

"This is the first time I've ever asked a woman if I could kiss her."

She pressed her soft curves and sweet-smelling warmth against him. "Did my answer surprise you?"

Yes. No. "A little."

"You know what surprises me?" she asked.

"What?"

"You've asked if you can kiss me and I've said yes, but you're still talking."

He took her face in his hands lowered his head till her lips were only a breath away. "Are you saying I'm all talk and no action?"

"Yes." She laughed. "That's what I'm saying."

Well, they couldn't have that, now could they? He kept his gaze on hers and took his time making contact. She kept her eyes open, too, and he liked that. He brushed his mouth lightly over hers and pulled back a little.

Her eyes went wide. "That was it? You call that a kiss?"

He liked that she could be playful without being coy. "What did you have in mind?"

"A little more effort." She curled her fingers around his biceps and he found himself hoping she was impressed. "You didn't even try to get to first base."

He played along with her. "On a first date? I didn't think you were that kind of girl."

She toyed with one of the buttons on his shirt. "I didn't say you'd get there."

He thought of her poring over his high-school yearbooks and all of a sudden he didn't feel so sure of himself. He remembered nice girls like Maggie. They were never the topic of testosterone-driven, locker-room bragfests because guys like him never went out with them. Looking back, it was more likely that they avoided guys like him.

His locker-room nickname had been "Hit Man." God, he hadn't thought about that in years, and for good reason. He'd been damned proud of it at the time but looking back...

He'd needed a good swift kick in the ass.

He wasn't a teenage Don Juan anymore and Maggie wasn't the

pretty-but-shy wallflower dating a guy in the chess club. She was a very grown-up, *very* sexy woman and she wanted him to kiss her.

He could definitely put some effort into that.

This time he waited until her eyes fluttered shut before he covered her mouth with his. After a few rounds of give-and-take stroking and nudging, her lips parted and the next thing he knew, her tongue was playing a sassy little game of hide-and-seek with his. Her hands were in his hair and her warm slender body was in full, no-holds-barred contact with his.

After years of thinking he knew everything there was to know about women, who knew nice girls could kiss like this? And if he did make a move, how far would she let him go?

Not far enough to satisfy him, but maybe far enough to wipe out any chance of them having a professional working relationship.

He eased back. "Maggie?"

Her eyelids went up halfway. "Mmm-hmm?"

He tried to catch his breath. "Did I get an A for effort that time?"

"A-plus." Her lips were a little fuller and a little redder, and when she ran her tongue over them, he wanted to kiss her all over again.

"Any chance you want to earn some bonus marks?" she asked.

"It's tempting but I'm kind of concerned about how we're going to work together after this."

With a wicked little smile, she touched her fingers to her lips, then his. "I have a feeling we're going to work very well together."

Then she let herself inside and closed the door, leaving him alone on her front porch, horny as hell. Letting her go that easily was a first for him, too.

MAGGIE CLOSED THE DOOR and did a little dance down the hallway to the kitchen.

Yes!

Yes, yes, yes!

She twirled around and flopped into a chair, then she jumped to her feet again and twirled some more.

Yes!

If she was never kissed again, it wouldn't matter.

Ha. Who was she kidding? She'd been born to be kissed by Nick Durrance. And she could think of a few other things she'd like him to do.

Tonight had gone well, she decided after mustering up a little perspective. In spite of Nick's reluctance to go to Allison's barbecue and his lack of confidence around family and old friends, he'd done just fine. And his self-confidence would gradually increase, she was sure of it. Until he didn't need her at all.

She replayed the kiss again. It would be nice if he still needed her, but just for different reasons.

Very personal reasons.

She hugged herself at the delicious thought of being personally needed by Nick Durrance.

In less than ten hours, he would be back to start construction. "I hope you don't mind me doing this, Aunt Margaret. This is a dream come true for me."

I'd say a few dreams came true tonight.

Maggie laughed. "I was talking about opening the spa, you sly old woman!" Making out with Nick was an unexpected bonus. "And you shouldn't have been spying on us."

I was not spying on you, young lady. Any fool could figure out what made you come whirling in here the way you did. Then she chuckled. *I say, good for him.*

Aunt Margaret had always assured her that someday the right man would come along and sweep her off her feet. He wouldn't love her in spite of her being an intuitive free spirit. He'd love her because of it.

"Is he the one you were talking about, Aunt Margaret?"

Silence.

"This is so typical." Her aunt had always been quick with the assurance and advice but disappeared when it was time to answer the hard questions.

"Are you going to answer my question?"

Still nothing.

"Fine, then, if that's how you want to be. But I love you, and I'll always be grateful for the chance to open my spa and help people."

Knowing Aunt Margaret, she'd turn up again when she was least expected. And the least helpful.

THE NEXT MORNING Nick and his crew—which turned out to be one other person —were twenty minutes early. Maggie met them at the front door. "Hi."

"Hi, yourself," Nick said. "We're a little early. I hope that's okay."

"Of course."

After last night's kiss, she'd wondered how she'd react to seeing him again —and how he'd react to her— but the man standing next to Nick on the front porch provided all the distraction they needed to get past that. And then some.

"This is Brent," he said. "He works for me."

Brent held out his hand. "The last name's Borden," he said. "In case you ever need to look me up in the phone book."

Maggie laughed and put her hand in his. "Nice to meet you."

Brent held on. "You have no idea."

Nick cleared his throat.

Brent grinned and let go "Dang. I promised the boss I'd behave but it looks like I'm already in hot water."

Maggie was going to enjoy this. Nick's one-man crew was heartbreakingly handsome, although it only took a few seconds to figure out that he didn't take anything—or anyone—seriously. Not even himself. He had his ball cap on backward and a belt buckle that appeared to double as a bottle opener. He reminded her of a big, boisterous puppy that was so adorable you didn't mind when it peed on the kitchen floor. She smothered a giggle and wondered if she'd get to know Brent well enough to share that with him.

Brent smiled. "Nick says you'll be spending a lot of time here during the construction."

"Yes, I will, but I'll try to stay out of your way as much as I can."

Brent's brazen gaze traveled over her. "You can get in my way all you like. I don't know about Nick, though." Then he gave his boss a sideways glance. "Think you can handle the distraction?"

Nick was not amused, but he definitely looked uncomfortable. Probably because of the kiss.

Hmm. Another kiss might be the best antidote for that.

Definitely.

For now, she'd let herself be distracted by Brent's outrageous flirting. His outgoing personality could fill up a room, although his good looks didn't overshadow Nick's, at least not in Maggie's opinion.

"If you're ready," Nick said, "we'll bring in our tools and get to work taking down that wall."

Maggie took a long breath and one last look around. "I took some pictures this morning. You know, the 'before' pictures for my scrapbook."

"Good idea," Nick said.

"Scrapbook?" Brent asked.

"Nick gave me a beautiful scrapbook to keep a record of the renovations. I'll put it on display when the spa opens."

"I didn't know that was company policy, but it's a good one."

Brent gave Nick a playful jab in the shoulder. "Always thinking, this guy. Guess that's why he's the boss and I just do what I'm told."

Nick glared at him. "Since you're so good at it, how 'bout you bring in those tools?"

"Yes, sir." Brent winked at Maggie, gave Nick a mock salute and sprinted down the steps, tripping on the loose tread on the second step. He caught himself before he hit the ground, then spun around and grinned up them. "I think I'd better fix that before somebody gets hurt."

Nick rolled his eyes. "He needs to worry about more than the front steps."

Maggie smiled as she watched Brent hoist a couple of tool-boxes out of the back of the truck. "He's very…energetic."

"And mostly harmless, although I try to keep him on a short leash."

She laughed and added a leash to her big-boisterous-puppy image of Brent.

"Glad you find him amusing but if he starts to get on your nerves, let me know."

"I'm sure we'll get along just fine."

Nick's eyes went narrow. "Yeah, well, just watch out. He can be a bit of a…" He shook his head.

"What?"

"Nothing." He turned away to check on Brent's progress with the toolboxes.

Nothing, indeed. It was kind of sweet that Nick didn't want him flirting with her. She smiled. A few days ago she wouldn't have hesitated to engage in a little harmless flirtation with a man like Brent. Now she had other things on her mind.

"Don't worry about me. I know his type. He's probably an Aquarius."

Nick shrugged. "You've got me."

"When's his birthday?"

"I'm pretty sure it's the end of January."

Maggie grinned. "That's Aquarius, all right. You can spot them a mile away."

Nick stared at her. "How do you do that?"

"What?"

"Figure people out so easily. You can tell when a total stranger was born. You always manage to say exactly what people want to hear."

"Yes, well, sometimes I tell them things they don't want to hear. I'm still learning when it's okay to say what's on my mind and when to keep it to myself."

"If you ever figure it out, I know a few people who would benefit from that lesson."

"To answer your question, I'm not sure. Aunt Margaret always said I have a gift. It's taken me a long time to understand what that means—and I'm not sure I do, completely—but I see things that people would rather I didn't see. I can see what makes them unhappy, even when they can't see it themselves, and I can help them fix it."

Nick looked skeptical. "You sound like my family."

She didn't really believe he meant that, but she'd better not say any more in case he got suspicious. "Really? You think I'm like your family?"

He looked confused. "No, of course not. You're nothing like my family."

Brent plunked two toolboxes on the front porch. "Thank heavens for that. When you meet his family, you'll know what I mean."

"I met Leslie at Allison's barbecue last night. She seemed very nice, and it was good to see that she and Nick get along so well."

Nick and Brent exchanged looks.

"Are you sure we're talking about the same person?" Brent asked. "Nick's sister? Leslie Durrance?"

"Of course. She's delightful. After Nick told her what a beautiful bride she's going to be, she said she was looking forward to seeing both of us again at the wedding. Isn't that right?"

Nick agreed. "Yeah, actually, that's pretty much the way it happened."

"Get out of town! Leslie said she was looking forward to seeing you at the wedding?"

Nick and Maggie both nodded.

"But she gave you a lecture, right? Told you what to wear? How to behave? How not to behave?"

Nick and Maggie shook their heads.

"Get out of town," Brent said again.

"In fact, before we left the party last night, she asked me if I'd walk her down the aisle."

"Get out of—"

Nick reached for one of the toolboxes. "Enough already. We're staying in town and I think it'd be a good idea if we got to work."

Maggie laughed.

Brent grabbed the handle of the other toolbox. "She really asked you to walk her down the aisle?"

"Yes."

"And your mother's okay with that?"

Nick shrugged. "You know something? I really don't care."

Brent's reaction to all of this was interesting, to say the least. So was Nick's. It was as though neither of them could believe that something positive could happen in Nick's family. But anything was possible, and Maggie wondered how long it would take Nick to figure that out.

TWO HOURS INTO the renovation, Maggie thought she'd go mad if she had to listen to another minute of the sound of hammers pounding and plaster falling and wood splintering. Even worse, she was having second thoughts—serious second thoughts—which was not like her at all.

Was this the right thing to do? What if this wasn't what Aunt Margaret had in mind when she'd left her house and all her money to Maggie?

But Aunt Margaret was not to be heard this morning. Which could only mean one of two things. Either the noise was too much for her, too, or she'd gone off in a huff.

Maggie ran upstairs and grabbed her bag. "I'll be back in a while," she yelled at Nick and Brent.

Acknowledgment came in the form of a brief nod from Nick as he made way for Brent, who was carrying a couple of discarded two-by-fours on his shoulder.

Maggie ducked beneath them and headed out the front door. She walked down the block and got all the way to the corner before the sounds of demolition faded. *Thank goodness,* she thought. She turned the corner and crossed the street to Donaldson's Deli.

The door jangled when she pushed it open and old Mr. Donaldson, who stood behind the counter slicing salami, glanced up at her. "G'morning, Maggie. I see you've started the work on your aunt's place."

Word traveled fast. "Yes. It's a lot noisier and messier than I thought it would be."

"Yep, that's to be expected. No pain, no gain." He shut off the slicer and stepped up to the counter. "What can I get for you this morning?"

The place smelled of fresh bread and sharp cheeses and spicy cold cuts. "A loaf of sourdough, please. And I'll need some stuff to make sandwiches."

"Well, if you're thinking about feeding those two construction workers of yours, then I'd suggest the Black Forest ham and Swiss cheese. It's Nick's favorite."

"You know what kind of sandwiches he likes?"

"I've been in business for forty-seven years next month. I can custom-make a sandwich for pretty near anybody in Collingwood Station. For Nick, I'd suggest the rye, though, instead of the sourdough."

Maggie hoped he'd be impressed when she produced his favorite at lunchtime. "Okay, I'll go with the ham and Swiss on rye. What about Brent Borden? What does he like?"

Mr. Donaldson peered over his bifocals. "That young man'll eat anything."

Maggie laughed. That didn't surprise her one bit.

"And should I wrap up some of this nice Havarti for you?"

"That's so sweet of you to remember."

"It's my job to remember. It was your aunt's favorite, too. God rest her soul." While he unwrapped a large ham and hefted it onto the slicer, Maggie studied the drinks in the cooler and tried to decide what to buy.

"Those two boys always like to have a beer with their lunch but I'd give them cola while they're on the job," Mr. Donaldson said over his shoulder.

Maggie grinned and grabbed the drinks. She could picture Nick and Brent perfectly, hammers in hand, tool belts riding low on their hips, tearing a wall out of her house.

Boys? I don't think so!

She set the bottles on the counter and dug her wallet out of her bag. "How much do I owe you?"

"Let's see. Enough food for two hungry carpenters and one pretty lady." He tipped his head back a little so he could see the cash register keys through his bifocals. "That'll be seven fifty."

She handed him the cash and reached for the bag. "Thanks, Mr. Donaldson."

"Anytime, my dear." He banged the drawer of the cash register shut. "How long do you figure this job is going to take?"

"Nick thinks it'll take about three weeks but I'm hoping they finish sooner."

"The important thing is that you're happy with it."

"I hope it's what Aunt Margaret wants— Would have wanted," she added quickly.

"Your aunt was always saying that she should have some work done on that place, especially after the rest of the neighborhood got all spruced up. But it's tough for old folks like us. We get set in our ways and we don't want anything to upset that."

"So you think she'd approve?"

"She thought the sun rose and set on you. She'd be darned proud, knowing you were moved in and fixing up the old place."

Maggie felt her worries float away. "Thank you, Mr. Donaldson. I needed to hear that."

He tipped his head to the side and smiled. "Oh, I almost forgot." He pulled three sticks of licorice from a glass jar near the cash register. "These are on the house. Those boys love licorice."

"THOSE BOYS" WERE STILL hard at work when Maggie returned to the house. What had once been a wall was a gaping hole and what had once been a living room was a pile of plaster and boards.

Nick swiped the back of his hand across his forehead. "I had to shut the power off. As soon as we disconnect this wiring, I'll switch it back on."

She stared at his dust-streaked T-shirt and tried to swallow. "No problem," she croaked. "I don't need to turn anything on."

Nick's mouth hinted at a smile, and she felt her face heat up.

"I'll just go put these things away." As she hurried through to the kitchen, she wished she was better at thinking about what she was going to say before she blurted it out.

She closed the fridge door and turned around to see a trail of plaster-dust footprints crisscrossing the kitchen floor. She'd better start using the back door. Not that she was a neat freak or anything, far from it, but this could quickly get out of hand. She grabbed the broom and was sweeping up when Nick came in.

"Turning the power back on." He disappeared down the back stairs to the basement where the electrical panel was located.

The refrigerator started to hum and the readout on the microwave blinked. "Thanks," she said when he reappeared. As she reset the clock, she sensed him move closer, then she could feel him standing behind her.

"Everything all right?" he asked.

She turned around, not expecting him to be as close as he was, but wishing he was even closer. "Of course. Why wouldn't it be?"

"You seem withdrawn, a little spooked even." He hesitated for a second or two. "Listen, if this is about last night—"

"No, it's not that." Not that she hadn't given last night a lot of thought.

"So what is it?"

She sighed. She'd felt better about this after talking to Mr. Donaldson, but now that she was back home in the noise and the dust, she was having second thoughts again. "These changes are happening so fast. You just got started and now that wall is already gone and I'm wondering what Aunt Margaret must be thinking about all of this."

His eyes widened a little. "How many Aunt Margarets do you have?"

"Just one."

"And she's dead. Right?"

"Yes, but she's still…you know." She waved both hands in the air.

Nick gave a nervous glance around the kitchen. "You're telling me that your deceased aunt—Miss Meadowcroft—is here in this kitchen?"

"Not right now. I don't know where she is. That's why I'm wondering if she's okay with all of this. Mr. Donaldson has known her for years and he told me this is what she would want me to do. But what if he's wrong? What if this isn't what she wants? What if she wants everything left just the way it was?"

He stared at her for a few seconds, as though he wasn't sure what to say. "You don't really think…" Then he shook his head. "Of course you do. Come here." He slid an arm around her shoulder and pulled her in close.

She went without hesitation and tucked her head beneath his chin, reassured by his warmth and just a little turned on by his construction-worker scent. A little voice in her head warned her that this was not a good idea, that Nick was one of those men who didn't fall in love with women like her, but in her heart she knew that none of that mattered.

"Let me tell you something," he said. "If your aunt is still hanging around and doesn't like what I'm doing, I'd be on my way to the hospital by now."

The idea of Aunt Margaret causing a mishap made her giggle. "So you believe me?"

"I believe you believe it, and that's good enough for me. As for the work we're doing, it's going to be noisy and dusty. There's no way around that."

"I know. Since I won't be able to keep experimenting with new products for the spa, I've decided to spend some time working on the garden. While we were at Allison's last night, I got a few ideas about what I'd like to do here. In fact, maybe I'll go over there right now and take another look, now that the party stuff has been cleared away."

"Good idea," he said. "And if you're over there, she won't be showing up here."

"True." She liked that he didn't want Allison around. Silly to feel that way, but it was the truth.

She looked up at him and he lowered his head a little.

She tilted her face toward his and let her lips part just ever so slightly.

She hadn't expected to kiss him so soon after last night but now that it was about to happen—

Brent cleared his throat. "Ah, boss?"

Maggie squirmed out of Nick's embrace. How long had Brent been watching from the doorway? Not that it should matter, but she didn't want him to think she was the kind of woman who threw herself at every man who came along. Nick was definitely an exception.

"What's happening?" Nick asked, calm as could be, as though they hadn't been caught in an almost-kiss.

"Out there?" Brent asked. "Nothing. In here? Very hard to say."

"Maggie was just telling me about her plans for the garden."

"Right. That would have been my first guess."

Maggie decided she didn't want to stick around to see where this conversation was going. "I'll head over to Allison's right now and let you get back to work. I'll be back at lunchtime. I hope you don't mind sandwiches."

"We don't expect you to make lunch for us every day," Nick said.

Brent loudly cleared his throat.

Nick rolled his eyes. "Let me amend that. *I* don't expect you to make lunch for us."

Brent was grinning now. "You'll have to excuse him. Poor upbringing. Doesn't understand that it's bad manners to turn down an invitation to lunch."

Maggie laughed. Brent's goofy sense of humor offset Nick's tendency to take things too seriously. "It's no trouble," she assured Nick. And it wasn't. She had an idea that Brent could provide a lot of insight into the things that were bothering Nick.

Chapter Eight

Maggie rang Allison's doorbell. While she waited, she contemplated the conservative brown-stained front door and decided she would paint hers red.

She rang the bell again.

Please let Allison be home, she thought. She really wanted a break from the noise at her place.

Just as she turned to leave, the door opened.

Allison's elegant little pale blue dress and white sandals were stunning. Her makeup was ghastly and the overdone eyeliner and thick mascara did a poor job of masking puffy, red eyes.

"Maggie, this is a nice surprise," she said with a complete lack of enthusiasm.

"I hope I'm not bothering you. Is everything all right?"

"Of course. Why do you ask?"

"Because you've been crying."

A hint of emotion flickered on Allison's face. "I'm a little tired, that's all. All the preparations for the party must have worn me out and I think I'm having an allergic reaction to something."

Maybe to a newly divorced woman who has the hots for your husband? Maggie wondered, recalling Nick's speculation about John and Candice.

"I can dash home and get some ephedra tea for you. It works wonders on allergies." Not that she was buying the allergy excuse.

"Oh, don't go to any trouble. I'll be fine."

"Are you sure? It's no trouble."

"I'm sure. But, where are my manners? Would you like to come in?"

Ever the perfect hostess. "Yes, thanks. I was hoping to visit for a while. The noise at my place is making me crazy, but if this is a bad time…"

"A visit would be nice. I could use some company."

Maggie knew Allison well enough to know this despondency was uncharacteristic. "What's wrong?"

"I'm being silly. I usually don't overreact to things but—" She burst into tears.

Oh, dear, Maggie thought. This was not good.

But she had a hunch about what was causing the distress and she knew she could help, if Allison would let her. "Let's go inside," she said. "I'll make some tea."

"You must think I'm a complete fool," Allison sobbed.

"Why would I think that? Something's obviously upsetting you."

In the kitchen she directed Allison to a chair in the breakfast nook that overlooked the deck where the bar had been set up last night. Early that morning Maggie had noticed a crew of young men hauling away the folding tables and chairs and now the yard showed no signs of the party that had been held there the night before.

"I'm so sorry. This isn't like me."

"Sit down," she said when Allison protested. She picked up a box of tissues off the counter and slid it across the table. While Allison dabbed at her eyes and gently blew her nose, Maggie filled the kettle and plugged it in. She kept up a steady stream of conversation, hoping to distract Allison from her problems until they could sit and talk about them face-to-face.

"Do you know Nick's friend Brent? They've made amazing progress this morning. They've already taken down one wall and started on the new bathroom. Can you believe it?"

She chose a package of chamomile tea from the pantry, found a couple of china cups and saucers and set them on the table.

"I didn't know I'd find the noise and commotion so overwhelming though. I mean, you'd think after living my whole life in New York that I'd be used to noise, but construction is different."

She rinsed a teapot with hot water and popped a couple of tea bags into it.

"There. Now, where was I? Oh, right. The noise. I had to get out of the house this morning so I walked over to the deli and bought everything I needed to make sandwiches for lunch. That'll be fun, I think. Brent is such a character. Do you know if he and Nick have been friends for a long time?"

Allison wiped her eyes with a fresh tissue. "Practically forever."

How she managed to mop up the tears without smudging all that makeup, Maggie would never know.

The kettle whistled and after she filled the pot, Maggie set it on a trivet next to the cups on the table. "It must be wonderful to have grown up with a best friend like that," she said as she took a seat.

"These days kids call them BFFs."

"Best friends…"

"Forever."

"Oh, I love that!" Maggie said. "I've had a few good friends over the years but people in the city tend to move around a lot, so I've never had a BFF."

She gave the pot a gentle swirl before she filled the cups. Her sixth sense was telling her that Allison's emotional turmoil involved Candice and John, which meant the talk about best friends was a perfect segue into getting her to talk about was bugging her. "What about you? Who were your best friends?"

Allison gazed into her tea, as though looking for the answer. "I had two," she said finally. "Candice and Leslie, although these days I'm not so sure about Candice."

Bingo.

Maggie reached for Allison's hand and gave it a squeeze. "You know what I think? I think John is one of your best friends, too. He's obviously crazy about you, and last night I could tell he was so proud of the way you arranged everything for the barbecue."

Allison plucked another tissue from the box, which suggested more tears were on the way. "You must have seen him with Candice. She was all over him."

The admission surprised Maggie. There was the difference between the polished and poised wife of a successful lawyer that Allison wanted the world to see, and the vulnerable young woman she was inside, filled with doubts and insecurity.

"I noticed." While Maggie was sure there was nothing going on between John and Candice, she did have the uneasy feeling that he could be tempted. "Did you talk to John about it?"

She shook her head and blew her nose again.

"Well, what I noticed was that he wasn't 'all over' her. I think he was just trying to be a gentleman and not embarrass her, but I'm sure he didn't mean to upset you."

Allison brightened a little. "You think so?"

"I do. And I think you should talk to him about it."

"I don't know. What if he tells me—" But Allison couldn't seem to bring herself to say whatever it was that she thought her husband might say.

"You really think John's interested in her when he has you, two great kids and this beautiful home?" She gestured with both hands.

"I'm not sure what I think anymore."

"Do you still think Candice is one of your best friends?"

"Maybe not," she answered cautiously.

"How many times has she been married?"

"Three."

How was it, Maggie wondered, that some women found so many marriageable men when she'd never been able to find one? "She doesn't seem very happy for a woman who's so popular with men." Not to mention filthy rich.

"She was devastated after her first divorce. Leslie and I felt terrible for her and we rallied around and did what we could to cheer her up. But in less than a year she was married again."

"How long did that one last?"

"About a year and a half. By then we were starting to think maybe the husbands weren't the problem."

No kidding. "How long have you and John been married?"

"Eight years."

"That's wonderful! Plus you have two great kids and a beautiful home. What makes you think he'd throw all this away for someone who goes through husbands faster than most of us wear out a pair of shoes?"

Allison smiled at that, then went serious again. "Lately, John and I seem to have gone our separate ways. He works late several nights a week. I'm busy with the kids' school and other activities. We don't spend much time together anymore."

"But there must be things you like to do as a family. And just the two of you."

She nodded. "We used to take the kids on picnics or to the zoo, but now we're always too busy."

Too busy to save your marriage? Maggie wondered. "I think you should tell John that you and the kids would like to spend more time with him."

"I don't know."

"I guarantee you it'll work like a charm."

"Speaking of charms, you've done wonders with Nick."

Hmm. "I don't have the faintest idea what you mean."

"Last week you said he'd make an interesting project. Remember? Whatever you're doing, it's working."

Even to her own ears, her high-pitched laugh sounded nervous. "I didn't mean anything by that. I think he's fine the way he is."

Allison set her cup on the table and leaned toward her. "Nick's definitely changed." Her voice sounded conspiratorial. "Like I said, whatever you've done—"

"I haven't done anything. I mean, he's dropped by a few times to talk about renovating my house, and then we went to your party last night, which we really enjoyed, by the way. I've never been to a catered barbecue before. It was very elegant. Anyway, then he walked me home and we—"

If you're going to tell her about your little make-out session last night, you might want to think again.

Aunt Margaret?

Allison was smiling, as though she'd just been let in on a secret.

Maggie felt her face turn red. "Sorry, I forgot what I was going to say." Ugh. She had to be the world's worst liar. And what on earth was Aunt Margaret doing over here?

"That's okay. I know what you were going to say. My lips are sealed." She twisted two fingers in front of her mouth, then flicked them over her shoulder. "Lately I've been wondering what my life would have been like if I'd stayed with Nick."

Excuse me? For once, Maggie couldn't think of anything to say. At least nothing appropriate. "Hands off my man" came to mind, but Nick wasn't hers.

Before she could summon up a coherent thought, Allison abruptly changed the subject. "Leslie called me this morning. You'll never guess what she's done."

"You mean about asking Nick to walk her down the aisle? He told me."

"I'm surprised he agreed. So is she. In fact, Leslie commented on how much he's changed." Allison studied her for a few seconds. "Maybe you really did work some magic on him."

Maggie shrugged. "I think he's honored that she asked."

"Well, you could have knocked me over with a feather. I asked what her mother thought of the idea, but Leslie hasn't told her yet. All I can say is that I would not want to be in her shoes right now."

"Well, it is her wedding."

Allison's arched eyebrows suggested otherwise. "Mrs. Durrance has the final say on everything that goes on in that family. Except with Nick. She gave up on him years ago."

"That's terrible!"

"The situation might not have been so bad if Nick had been a little more cooperative."

Or if he'd tried to be somebody he wasn't. "He seems really pleased that Leslie asked him to do this for her, but Brent was just as surprised as you are."

"Well, that's a whole other story."

"What do you mean?"

"If Nick ruins Leslie's wedding, Brent Borden will be the happiest man on earth."

"I've only just met Brent, but he doesn't strike me as being that mean-spirited." As for the remark about Nick, she wouldn't even dignify that with a response.

"You would have no way of knowing this, but Brent has been head-over-heels for Leslie for as long as any of us can remember. I'm sure that's why he stayed friends with Nick all these years."

"Their friendship seems pretty genuine to me." Besides, if Nick and Leslie weren't close, how would that help Brent?

Maggie, my dear, do not try to put yourself in the heads of these small-minded people. It's not someplace you want to be.

For once Aunt Margaret's wry sarcasm was welcome.

"It hardly matters what Brent's been thinking," Allison said. "Leslie's fiancé is handsome and respectable, not to mention very wealthy. Between Gerald's money and hers, they're set for life."

"I met him last night. He seems nice." But even if she factored in his bank balance, she wouldn't call him handsome. Especially not compared to Nick or Brent. She was tempted to remind Allison that good looks and respectability were often just a thin veneer, but something kept her quiet.

Are you paying attention, Aunt Margaret? I'm being very careful with what I say.

Humph.

"Leslie's goal was always Harvard law school and she never lost sight of it. If there was an award for overachievers, she'd win hands down. Brent chased her for years but she refused to have anything to do with him, and who could blame her? I mean, look at them now. She's a successful lawyer and he's just a construction worker."

"But it's what's inside that makes a person who they really are. I mean, you wouldn't have married John if you hadn't known he was a good person, would you?"

For a moment Allison seemed at a loss for words. "I'm sorry. That must have sounded incredibly shallow. I just meant that Leslie's chosen a husband as carefully as she chose a career. I'm sure everything will work out perfectly for her. It always does."

"You could be right."

She'd be right if the girl was buying a car.

Much as she longed to repeat Aunt Margaret's observation, Maggie kept it to herself. "I only know that Nick is pleased to be part of his sister's wedding, no matter who she's marrying."

"And that's where you come in."

"What do you mean?"

"He asked you to the wedding, then he introduced you to his sister, and the next thing we know he's in the wedding party. Do you think you can work some of that magic of yours on me and John?" Allison's spirits seemed to have brightened a little. "Maybe you and your mother can do one of your love spells for me and make everything all right."

Maggie drank the rest of her tea. Even though she could tell Allison wasn't serious, it wasn't a bad idea. Not a bad idea at all.

"I'm afraid I don't have a magic wand." What she did have, though, was a mother in Manhattan who would know exactly what she could do to fix her friend's marriage. "But a love spell…"

"You're not serious?"

"Well…"

Oh, she's serious all right. As a heart attack.

Very funny.

Allison was staring at her, waiting for an answer.

"No, of course not." The world was full of doubting Thomasinas but Maggie could work around that. What Allison didn't know wouldn't hurt her. "I do think you should talk to your husband. My parents always said that a solid relationship was built on communication. Talking to John will make you feel a lot better than imagining terrible things that will probably never happen."

"I'll think about it," Allison said cautiously.

"Always trust your instincts." And leave the magic to me. Maggie smiled, trying not to feel too smug. Gabriella would know exactly what she needed to do to save Allison's marriage.

She glanced at the clock and jumped up. "It's nearly lunchtime. I should get going. Will you be all right on your own?"

Allison stood, too. "Of course. Thank you for dropping by. I feel much better."

As Maggie gazed through the French doors one more time, she remembered the conversation she'd had with Nick's friends. "You really do have a lovely yard. Have you and John ever thought of building a tree house for the kids?"

"A tree house?"

"That big old oak in the corner of your yard would be a perfect place for a great big tree house."

"I've never given it any thought. What made you think of that?"

Maggie was quickly coming to the conclusion that the biggest problem with the people of Collingwood Station was that they had no imagination. "Kids love tree houses," she said with a shrug. "And I'll bet it'd make a fun family project." As long as no one worries about being sued.

Allison looked at the tree as though she were seeing it for the first time. "I don't know."

"Something to think about." Maggie glanced at the clock again. "I'll see you later. And, thanks. I really appreciate the break from the construction noise."

"Maggie?"

She looked back and waited.

"You won't say anything to anyone…you know…about the things we talked about?"

Good grief. Did Allison think she was going to become one of the local gossips? "Never! Everything we talked about this morning stays between us."

AFTER LUNCH, Maggie waited until Nick and Brent were preoccupied with demolishing another wall before she carried the cordless phone into the kitchen and dialed the number of her mother's shop in Greenwich Village.

"Hi, Gabriella. It's me," she said when she heard her mother's voice.

There was a momentary silence. "Maggie? Is everything okay?"

"Of course. Why wouldn't it be?"

"Why don't you tell me?"

"Everything is fine. How's the city?"

Her mother laughed. "Surely you haven't already forgotten how glorious summertime in Manhattan can be. It's hotter than hell and the humidity is through the roof."

"I haven't forgotten." She could picture her mother perfectly, sitting in her high-backed wicker chair in the back room, with the burgundy-velvet drapes pulled back. The drapes would be closed if she was with a client, but Gabriella wouldn't have taken the call if she was doing a reading. Right now she was probably lounging in the chair and fanning herself because the shop's stout-hearted but geriatric air conditioner never managed to produce enough cold air to reach the back room.

"But that's not why you called, is it?"

"Not really."

"And you don't miss this city, do you?"

Maggie had been way too busy to miss it. "No, I don't. But I miss you."

"Of course you do, darling. And I miss you like crazy. Now tell me about life in Sleepy Hollow."

Gabriella had only visited Collingwood Station once, years ago. She had declared it to be too provincial for words and had never gone back. After that one visit, Maggie had always come alone on the train to visit Aunt Margaret.

"Collingwood Station is a wonderful place to live. Even better than I expected. In fact, I don't think it could be any better than it is."

"So why are you calling?"

"Can't I just call to say hello?"

Her mother laughed. "My darling girl, you've always marched to the beat of your own drum. It's one of the things I love most about you. When you take on something, it's the only thing on your mind. Since I'm on your mind, you must need my help with something."

"Well, now that you mention it, I could use a little advice."

"What is it? Your project? How's it going?"

"Project?" Maggie leaned around the corner and looked down the hallway. Nick was coming through the front door with a couple of boards balanced on one shoulder, his dust-streaked T-shirt straining across his chest.

"Maggie? Are you still there? I asked about the spa. How's it going?"

"Oh. You meant the renovations."

There was more laughter. "Of course that's what I meant. What did you think I was talking about? Have you taken on another project?"

How much should she tell her mother? It wasn't that Gabriella would object to her interest in Nick. It's just that she would have all sorts of advice. And while Maggie needed to find a way to help Allison fix her marriage, she preferred to keep Project Nick to herself.

"Since you haven't answered, I assume that's a yes," her mother said. "Does he have a name?"

"I can't really talk about it right now. But I do need some advice about the woman next door. She's in a bit of a… situation and she needs my help."

"Did she ask for your help?"

"Mom! What kind of question is that?"

"A perfectly valid one, especially since you only call me Mom when you're trying to hide something."

"You're my mother. I can call you Mom if I want to. And yes, she asked for my help. She thinks her marriage is in trouble and she asked if I knew of any love spells."

"Was she serious?"

No. "Yes. Sort of. I was very careful to tell her that spells were out of my realm and I didn't tell her about you because I didn't want to get her hopes up, but I'm sure you'll know what to do to fix this."

"Darling, I'd love to come up and see you and meet your friend, but summer is always the busiest time in the shop. I can't even think of getting away before the middle of September."

That was two and a half months away. Left to their own devices, there was no telling what kind of trouble the two of them could create for themselves. What had Allison said? *Lately I've been wondering what my life would have been like if I'd stayed with Nick.*

Maggie leaned around the corner again, just in time to see Nick hoist a board over his head and nail it into place. She strengthened her resolve. No way was she going to let Allison interfere with Project Nick. "You could give me the instructions and I could do the spell."

There was no missing the caution in Gabriella's voice. "I don't know, darling. You've never shown any aptitude in this area."

Good grief. She communicated with Aunt Margaret every day. How difficult could it be to scatter some powder around and recite a chant?

"Maggie?"

"Yes?"

"I know what you're thinking, and it's not that easy. These spells are very powerful and if anything were to go wrong—"

Jeez, what was the worst that could happen? "Tell me exactly what to do and I'll follow your instructions to the letter."

Gabriella's sigh suggested she was close to giving in. "Why

don't you explain your neighbor's situation? I need to know what has to be done before I can say which spell we'll need to use."

Yes! This was going to work! Allison would stop thinking she'd made a mistake when she'd dumped Nick all those years ago and she and John would work things out. Maggie filled her mother in on Allison's problems.

"My God," her mother said. "I take back what I said about Sleepy Hollow. You're living in Peyton Place."

"Gabriella! It's not that bad." Although, after seeing Candice in action last night, she'd been kind of thinking the same thing. "Besides, people in the city have affairs, too."

"Yes, well, eight million other people provide a certain anonymity. And it always seems more sordid when white picket fences are involved."

Maggie laughed. "It's really not as bad as you make it out to be." Her mother was right about one thing though. Nothing in Collingwood Station stayed secret for long.

"Fine, I'll have to take your word for it until I can get up there and check out the place. Now, are you sure that John is really Allison's true love?"

"Allison believes he is."

"I'm asking what you believe."

Maggie gave that some thought. "You know, when I see them with their children, I think they make a perfect family. But when John and Allison are together without the kids, they seem kind of cool toward each other. I don't think it's so much that they don't love each other anymore. They've just sort of drifted apart."

"And what about the affair?"

"I don't think it's gone that far yet. Nick thinks it has, but I'm pretty sure John hasn't been unfaithful." Yet.

"That's my girl. Always trust your instincts. By the way, who's Nick?"

"Oh. He's my contractor."

"And he has an opinion about this?"

"He grew up here and his sister is...oh, never mind. It's complicated."

Gabriella was silent for a few seconds. "I'll bet it is. Tell me about Candice. Is she happy with her life?"

"Not at all," Maggie said without hesitation. "She's desperately searching for something and can't seem to find it. She has heaps of money but that doesn't seem to help."

"It never does. Well, my dear, I'm afraid to say it but I'm not sure that one spell is going to be enough. Getting your friends John and Allison to fall in love again is an easy matter, but if we want to be absolutely certain that this will be a success, we need to get this Candice person out of the picture. The best way to do that is use another spell that will help her find what she's looking for."

Maggie perked up. Two spells? This was going to be even more fun than she'd anticipated. "So you're going to let me do them?"

"I don't think we have a choice. If you're going to help these people, you have to do it now."

Gabriella was all business now. For the next fifteen minutes, she gave painstakingly precise instructions for preparing and carrying out the two love spells. Then, just to be safe, she made Maggie repeat everything she'd written down.

"I'm still nervous about this," she said. "Promise me you'll be careful?"

"Of course. Thanks, Gabriella. I wish you could have come up here to do them yourself, but this is the next best thing."

"You'll let me know how it goes?"

"Of course. I love you."

"I love you, too, darling girl, and I miss you terribly. But I have a feeling you're the best thing that's happened to that town in a long time."

Maggie disconnected and was rereading the notes she'd made in her notebook when Nick came in.

She slammed the book shut.

"What's up?" he asked.

"Nothing." She could tell he wasn't convinced. "Do you need something?"

He was still eyeing her notebook. "I thought you should take a look at where we're putting the new wall and make sure it's going to work for you."

"Oh. Of course." She tucked her notebook into a drawer and followed him into the construction zone.

At the entrance to her new bathroom, she took a good look around. Then she closed her eyes.

"Something wrong?" Nick asked.

She shook her head. "I'm just picturing how it's going to look when it's finished."

"Oh."

And it was going to be perfect. Gleaming porcelain. Wicker baskets stuffed with fluffy white towels. The soaker tub filled with lavender-scented water.

Nick reclining in the tub.

She opened her eyes and met his gaze. "How soon will we…will I…be able to use it?"

"Should be finished next week."

"That soon? You work fast."

He gave her an odd look and for one crazy heartbeat, she wondered if he'd known what she'd been thinking. His dark eyes were hard to read but if she had to guess, she'd say he was still thinking about the kiss they'd shared last night.

The sound of Brent's boots on the front steps made her back away. "I should let you get back to work."

Back in the kitchen, she gazed out the window at the house next door, knowing she was doing the right thing by helping Allison and John. And Candice. And Nick, indirectly.

She knew what Gabriella thought about most people who

lived here, but Nick was different. What would her mother think of him?

There was no question about what the people of Collingwood Station would think of her mother and the love spells. Aunt Margaret had always fostered Maggie's ability to connect with people and to understand what was going on with them. People skills, she'd called them. But she thought Gabriella's so-called psychic abilities were beyond flaky.

That's because they are, and you should know better than to waste your time with this nonsense.

"Don't even start with me, Aunt Margaret. I know what I'm doing. So does my mother."

Sometimes you don't have a lick of common sense between the two of you.

Humph. "We do so."

Chapter Nine

Three days into the project, Nick was thinking it was probably the best job he'd taken in a long time. Maybe ever. Once Maggie overcame her initial uncertainty about the noise and disruption, she'd become completely enthusiastic about the changes and the progress they were making. Lunch, which she insisted on preparing for them, had become his favorite part of the day. It was just sandwiches and lemonade, served picnic-style in the back-yard, but somehow she made it special. Even Brent was on his best behavior, and that was saying something.

And, of course, there were those incredible cookies. One of these days he really ought to ask about her secret ingredient, except he wasn't sure he wanted to know. He kind of liked the idea of her working some kind of magic on them.

He measured the opening for the bathroom window and double-checked the dimensions of the new window. It was one of the old stained-glass windows they'd salvaged from a previous renovation. It was exactly the color she wanted and only a tad too big. He reached for a plane.

Once he installed the window, he'd call it a day. The downside of spending all day here and having lunch with Maggie was having to go back to his apartment and eat a solo dinner that went from the freezer to the microwave to the table in under five minutes. He liked eating lunch with Maggie, and dinner would be even better.

Breakfast, too, for that matter.

Yeah, right. If dinner was a date, and dating a client was a bad idea, then factoring in breakfast was not a good plan.

He was planing the window frame and imagining how one of Maggie's omelets might taste when there was a knock at the front door. Brent had gone to the warehouse to pick up more supplies and Maggie was out shopping, so he set down his tools and opened the door. Allison's husband was the last person he expected to find on the other side.

"John. Hey, how's it going?"

"Great," John said, extending his hand.

The guy obviously didn't know a lot of construction workers, and Nick didn't want to seem rude so he dusted his hand on his jeans and shook John's hand. "If you're here to see Maggie, she's—"

"No, I came over to talk to you. Do you have a minute?"

"Yeah, sure. What's up?"

"Well, Allison's suddenly got this idea that we should build a tree house for the kids, but I don't know anything about carpentry."

"You're looking for a contractor to build a tree house?"

John laughed. "No, I just need some advice. Allison seems to think it'll be a great family project."

"I see," Nick said, but he wasn't sure he did. What was it that Maggie had said to Jocelyn and Francine at the barbecue on Sunday?

If I had kids and this was my yard, I'd build a tree house in the arms of that big old oak.

How did she do this? She only had to mention something and the next thing he knew, people were going along with it. Not that a tree house was a bad idea. It was just out of character for John and Allison. Had Maggie suggested it, or were they under her spell the way everyone else in this town seemed to be?

"What I'm wondering," John said, somewhat tentatively, "is if you can tell me what kind of tools and materials I might need."

"Sure, no problem. What kind of tree house do you have in mind?"

John gave him a blank stare. "Ah—"

"You could start at the lumber yard," Nick suggested. "They might have books with plans and supply lists."

"Oh, good idea." But he didn't sound convinced.

"Tell you what, after you and Allison and the kids decide what you want, bring the plans over and I'll take a look. I'll be happy to lend you some tools and we've got plenty of scrap lumber around. You can help yourself to whatever you need."

John looked a little more enthusiastic. "Thanks, Nick. I appreciate it." And he sounded like he meant it.

"Happy to help."

"I should be getting back." John turned to leave.

"Good for you for taking this on," Nick said. "I wish my father and I had done something like this."

"Me, too," John said.

They stood there for a few seconds, unsure of what to say next.

Nick shifted his weight from one foot to the other.

John stuffed his hands into his pockets. "I'd better get home. Allison wants me to keep the kids occupied while she makes dinner."

"Yeah, and I should get back to work."

John left, and Nick picked up the plane and went back to work on the window. He had no idea what had made him reveal those feelings about his father. Growing up, it had never occurred to him that other kids' fathers were too busy to spend time with them. Looked as though he and John had more in common than he'd thought.

John's domestic situation sounded good though. Spend some

time with the kids. Have a nice dinner. Go to bed with the woman you'd shared it with.

Maybe he *should* ask Maggie if she'd like to go out for dinner.

Nah. Bad idea. As long as he was working for her, he needed to keep their relationship strictly professional. Going out for dinner would lead to more kissing, and that was not a place they needed to be right now.

"Hey, boss." Brent barged through the front door with a bag of mortar on one shoulder. "You want to give me a hand unloading those tiles? Then I think it's time we called it a day."

Nick glanced at his watch. "You're right. After we unload that stuff and tidy up, do you want to grab a burger at Paul's Place? Maybe shoot some pool?"

"Sure. You buying?"

Nick jabbed him in the shoulder. "Hey, on your salary you should be buying me dinner."

"I'll buy if you ask Maggie to come with us."

"She's not here."

"Dang," Brent said. "I was thinking it could be my lucky day."

"Yeah, well, dream on. Besides, I don't think it's a good idea."

"Because?"

"I just don't."

Brent muttered something that sounded a lot like, "That's got to be a first."

Nick decided to ignore it. After they'd put everything away and swept up the wood shavings and drywall dust, he locked up and they headed out to the truck. As they pulled away from the curb, he spotted Maggie walking up the sidewalk toward them.

She looked great. She had on a pair of calf-length jeans with the cuffs rolled up and a tank top in her trademark purple, which was never a color he'd thought he liked until he'd seen it on her.

"Pull over," Brent said as he rolled down the window.

Maggie had her arms full of packages, but she smiled and nodded a greeting.

Nick stopped the truck.

"Want to join us for dinner?" Brent asked. "We're going down to Paul's for a burger and a game of pool."

Jeez, Nick thought. What part of "it's not a good idea to invite Maggie for dinner" did Brent not understand?

"Oh, I can't. Not tonight. It sounds like fun but I sort of have plans." She angled her head, looked into the cab at Nick and smiled.

Nick told himself he shouldn't feel disappointed by her answer—after all, it had been his idea to *not* invite her.

"Too bad," Brent said. "Maybe next time."

"Definitely. It's a date." She shifted her packages into one arm and waved. "See you guys tomorrow."

Nick gave her a brief nod as he pulled away. Not that it was any of his business, but he'd sure like to know what her "sort of" plans might be.

BY THE END OF THE WEEK, Maggie was looking forward to the weekend and having two whole days of peace and quiet. The renovations were very distracting. She hadn't experimented with any new beauty products and her plans to work in the garden had fallen by the wayside. But she had kept herself busy rereading Gabriella's instructions and gathering the things she needed for the love spells.

The spell for Allison and John was the most important so she'd prepare that one first. She'd needed a few of John's hairs from his hairbrush, so midweek she'd paid Allison another visit. Luckily the children had been home and Meredith had wanted to take her upstairs to see her new dollhouse. While Meredith was occupied, she'd snuck into the master bedroom. After a moment of panic, she'd found John's hairbrush next to his sink in the en suite. At least she assumed it was his sink, since the other one was surrounded by an enormous number of expensive creams and lotions. She really must convince Allison to use more natural skin-care products.

She'd plucked a bunch of hairs from John's brush and quickly examined them before folding them into a small piece of paper and tucking it into the back pocket of her jeans.

Tonight she'd have to figure out some way to get back in to slip the spell under their bed. But first she had to make it.

She carefully measured spices and sugar into the beautiful little heart-shaped jar she'd decided to use. Her mother's instructions hadn't specified what kind of container but this one seemed perfect. She put the stopper in the opening and shook it to mix the spices. The blend of sugar and spice made her think of the giant cinnamon buns that Mr. Donaldson sold at his deli every morning.

She uncorked a bottle of rose water and took a sniff. Mmm. One her favorite scents. She slowly poured the liquid into the jar, closed the stopper and gently shook it again. Now for the hair. She unfolded the paper and studied the contents. She tried to slide the hair off the paper and into the jar, but the opening was too small. She was reluctant to actually touch the hair but she had no choice, so she quickly dumped them into her palm.

Ew, ew, ew.

But also kind of interesting. Some of them were definitely gray. Poor John. His hairline was receding *and* he was going prematurely gray. If Nick's yearbook pictures were anything to go by, his hair still looked as good now as it had ten years ago.

She checked the instructions and found that the amount of hair wasn't specified so she stuffed all of it into the jar. She pushed in the stopper and gave the jar one final shake. Some of the spices had formed little clumps in the rose water and the hair looked completely gross. She set the jar aside and read the rest of the instructions.

Apply a sweet-smelling oil to the outside of the jar.

She decided to use lavender.

Tie a yellow ribbon around the jar.

Done.

Put the jar under the couple's bed.

That was the tricky part.

After retrieving a light jacket that had pockets big enough to hold the jar, she slipped the jar into a little plastic bag, tucked it into her pocket, then let herself out the front door and headed for Allison's. She didn't exactly know how she'd get upstairs and into the bedroom but she'd play it by ear.

What makes you think this is going to work?

Aunt Margaret! Always the skeptic. "My mother wouldn't recommend a spell that doesn't work. But even if it doesn't, what's the worst thing that can happen?"

You get caught crawling around under people's beds?

She could picture her aunt's eye roll. "I'm not going to get caught and when this spell works, you'll have to eat those words."

We'll see about that.

"Yes, we will, won't we?" She rang Allison's doorbell, hoping Aunt Margaret didn't plan to follow her inside.

John answered the door and he seemed surprised to see her. "Maggie. What can I do for you?"

"Hi, John. I came over to see Allison. Is she here?"

"Sorry. She dropped kids off at her mother's place and went to help Leslie with wedding plans."

"I see."

"Do you need something?"

"No, but I was wondering…" *Come on, Maggie. Use your head. If you want to help Allison, you have to think of a way in.*

"Um, the last time I was here, Meredith took me upstairs to see her dollhouse and while I was up there I noticed the way you've fixed up your main bathroom and you probably know I'm renovating my place so I wondered—"

"You want to look at our bathroom?" He sounded confused.

"Yes! If that's okay with you. If it isn't, I can come back when Allison's home but I was sort of hoping—"

"Be my guest. You'll have to excuse me, though. I have to finish up some paperwork."

"Thanks." She dashed upstairs before he could change his mind. At the top of the staircase, she glanced back to be sure John wasn't watching.

No sign of him. *Maggie, you are a genius.*

She slipped into the bedroom, fished the jar out of her pocket and crouched next to the bed. *I really hope there's nothing under here I'm not supposed to see,* she thought.

She lifted the edge of the bed skirt and took a peek. Nothing but a few dust bunnies. Not that Allison would want anyone to know about those, but at least they were better than some things people kept under their beds. She slid the jar as far under as she could and straightened the bed skirt, hoping the scent of lavender would have dissipated by the time they went to bed.

"Everything okay up there?"

Holy crap! His voice was far enough away that she'd guess he was still downstairs. She crawled to the door on her hands and knees and peeked into the hallway. No sign of him.

"Maggie?"

"Yes, hi! Everything's fine." From where she knelt by the door, he wouldn't be able to see her from the bottom of the stairs. But if she stood now, he'd wonder what she was doing in the bedroom. Her only option was to crawl down the hallway to the main bathroom, where she was supposed to have been all along. She scooted along, listening for footsteps on the stairs.

She glanced over her shoulder, crawled into the bathroom and got to her feet. Then, trying to control her breathing, she casually leaned out the door. "I'm just making a few notes. I'll be right down."

The main bathroom was decorated in white and candy-striper pink. Aside from being too girlie, it was one of the most uninspired rooms she'd ever seen. Exactly what she *didn't* want in her house. She splashed some cold water on her face and tried to steady her nerves. Then she went downstairs. No sign of her host. "Thanks, John," she called from the front door.

He came out of the den. "What did you think?"

"Nice. Very nice."

He looked skeptical. "Really?"

Maggie laughed. "You don't like pink?"

"It wouldn't have been my first choice."

"Mine, either." Ugh. Dumb thing to say. How was she going to get out of that? "You have a great soaker tub. Nick is putting one in for me and I've never really looked that closely at one and I wasn't sure how big it was so I thought if I had another look at yours then I'd have a better idea of what to expect when mine's installed."

John quirked his eyebrows at her but he didn't say anything.

"Sorry. I have a tendency to talk too much when I'm—" Nervous. But she couldn't say that. "Excited. About soaker tubs. And…you know, decorating."

John was staring at her as though he thought she needed medication.

"I should let you get back to work."

"I'll tell Allison you dropped by."

"Thanks." She darted out the door and headed across the lawn to her place. She could hardly wait to tell Aunt Margaret that the plan had worked and she hadn't been caught, and now—

She stopped. Nick's truck was parked in front of her house. Why would he be here on Friday night? When he and Brent had left that afternoon, she could have sworn he'd said, "See you on Monday."

She found him in the new bathroom, tape measure in hand. He was still wearing his work clothes and his dark hair fell over his forehead, begging to be straightened.

Her fingers twitched.

Not tonight, she reminded herself. *You still have work to do.*

He glanced up. "Hi. Where've you been?"

"Nowhere."

"Nowhere?" His doubtful look made her squirm. "When I was a kid my father would always say, 'The lost-in-oblivion kind of nowhere or the I've-got-something-to hide kind of nowhere?'"

"I'm not hiding anything. I went for a walk. What would I have to hide?"

"Hey. Just making conversation."

"Oh. Well, so was I." She stuffed her hands into the pockets of her jacket and encountered the plastic bag, damp with lavender oil, that had held Allison and John's love spell.

Nick leaned toward her, close enough for her to touch his hair, if she dared. Did she?

"You smell great," he said.

She knew that look. It was exactly the same way he'd looked at her on Sunday night after he walked her home from Allison's, right before he'd asked if he could kiss her. This time she didn't think he'd ask. And she didn't want him to. She wanted to slide into his arms, pick up right where they'd left off and take each other places they'd nearly gone a few times this week. Almost certainly would have if Brent hadn't kept interrupting them.

But not tonight, she reminded herself again. Much as she'd love to take advantage of Brent's absence, she couldn't. She had to finish the other spell.

She stepped back.

There was no mistaking Nick's disappointment.

She stripped off the jacket and rolled it into a ball. "I was experimenting with an essential oil for a new shower gel. I must have spilled some on my jacket before I went out. For a walk. I'd better go put it in the laundry."

Walking away wasn't easy, especially since she could feel his gaze follow her as she rushed down the hallway to the kitchen.

She shook out the jacket and hung it on the back of a kitchen chair while she tried to sort out her thoughts. Nick might have come here with the intention of checking the measurements in the bathroom, but he also had other things on his mind.

The same things that were on her mind.

Obviously he'd known she was up to something. He'd been acting that way all week, but she was absolutely certain she hadn't done anything to tip him off.

Had she?

No way. He'd never figure out what she was doing.

Not in a million years.

Don't be so sure. These crazy things have a way of coming back to bite you on the—

"Aunt Margaret, this isn't that big a deal," she whispered. "Besides, it has nothing to do with Nick." Unless you counted salvaging Allison's marriage so she didn't complicate Nick's life by deciding to make a play for him. So although Maggie was doing this for Allison, not him, her success would still work to his advantage.

This kind of meddling always leads to no good.

"I'm not meddling," she whispered. "I'm helping." But right now she didn't feel like arguing with Aunt Margaret. As soon as Nick left, she had another spell to prepare.

She went back to the front of the house to see what Nick was doing. He was jotting notes on his clipboard.

"Can you hold the end of the tape measure against this wall?" he asked.

She held the little metal tab firmly against the wall while he extended the tape to the other side of the room. She was about to let her end go after he read the measurement, but he shook his head.

"Hold on."

So she held her end against the wall and as he moved toward her, the tape retracted into its case. And then he was standing right there in front of her. She had her back up against the wall and as he eased the end of the tape out of her fingers, she could feel the warmth of his body.

"I think I like being reeled in," he said.

"You do?"

His smile did interesting things to her insides and some of her outsides, too.

He lowered his head. "I do."

"We should finish measuring."

"I have all the measurements I need."

He hooked the tape measure on his belt and lowered his head toward hers. His mouth was inches from hers and about to make contact.

There's one more really important thing, Maggie. Because these spells are so closely connected, you'll have to do them at the same time for them to be really effective.

Surely she had time for a kiss. Just one nice, long delicious kiss. Which would lead to another, longer kiss. She was already a little breathless, just thinking about it. "Is there anything else you need?"

"Yeah."

Oh, my. She wanted this. Really wanted it. And he was even closer now, but still not touching her. He smelled like hard work and sawdust, and she could imagine leading him upstairs and stripping away his work clothes and climbing into the shower with him.

She closed her eyes. Yes, there was a very good chance that's what one kiss would lead to.

No way, she told herself. *Not tonight.* Nick would keep till tomorrow.

"So, how much longer do you think this is going to take?" she asked. "I mean, is there other stuff you need to do here tonight?"

He backed away. "I guess not. I've arranged for a plumber to come first thing Monday morning, so I want to get the new tub installed tomorrow, if that's okay. But if my being here is a problem—"

"Not really." She stifled a fake yawn. "It's been a long week, though, and I'm kind of tired and I have some…um…stuff to do."

If there was an Olympic record for making oneself scarce, Nick broke it.

She really hadn't wanted to make him leave, especially not in a snit, but this was her only opportunity to cast the spell for Candice. Tomorrow, when he came back to install the tub, they'd have plenty of time to pick up where they'd left off tonight. She'd whip up some lemonade and bake a fresh batch of chocolate chip cookies and they'd take it from there.

Tonight she still had to work some magic.

THE FIRST THING she needed was a photograph of Candice. She went upstairs to get the yearbook from Nick and Allison and Candice's senior year. Although it was more than ten years old, it was all she had.

Maggie opened the book to the *B*s. Candice's last name was Bentley-Ferguson, but in the yearbook it was just Bentley. Ferguson must have been contributed by one of the husbands. She'd been quite pretty in high school, although she hadn't been cover-model gorgeous like Allison had been, and still was. Maggie turned the page to find Nick's photo, then quickly flipped back.

She needed to focus, not daydream about being Nick's high-school sweetheart.

She took the book down to the kitchen and set it on the table, assembling the rest of the things she needed. Five red candles. Pink glass candle holders. Honey, icing sugar, cinnamon.

She smeared one of the candles with honey, sprinkled it with sugar and cinnamon and set it in the holder. By the time she'd coated the fifth candle, her hands were a sticky mess. On her way to the sink, she couldn't resist having a taste.

"Yum." Then she quickly washed her hands and hoped that sampling the spell wouldn't confuse the spirits.

After she cleared away the honey pot and the other ingredients, she spread a white lace cloth over the table and set the yearbook, open to Candice's picture, in the center. She hesitated.

Should she cut Candice's picture out of the book?

She ruled out that idea. Aunt Margaret had always had a thing about books. For an English teacher, it probably went with the territory. Books were not to be defaced. A yearbook was not great literature, but a book was a book and Maggie didn't want Aunt Margaret to be any more ticked off than she already was.

Should she cover the other photographs on the two open pages?

"Come on, Maggie," she said to herself. "Give the spirits a little credit. It's not like there arc any other Candices on this page."

The open yearbook wouldn't lie flat so she set the candles on the table around the whole book instead of immediately around the picture. Then she pulled the curtains closed and turned out the light.

Matches. She didn't have any matches.

She turned the light back on and rummaged through three kitchen drawers before she found some. She should have been better organized. She turned off the light again, struck a match and touched it to the first wick. The small circle of light cast a mysterious glow that made her smile.

This was more like it.

This was going to work.

The second candle lit and she moved the match to the third one.

"Ow!" She dropped the match and popped her singed fingers into her mouth, knocking over the first candle in the process.

"Damn it." Then she cast a look around. "Sorry," she said in case anyone was listening.

She quickly righted the candle. Fortunately both it and the match had been extinguished without doing any damage. There was a streak of honey and sugary cinnamon across the page, but that didn't seem like the end of the world. She wiped it up with a damp cloth, rearranged the candles and reached for the matches. This time she used a separate match for each candle and managed to light them all without mishap.

"Okay, now we're getting somewhere."

She closed her eyes, took a couple of long, deep breaths and tried to settle herself into a meditative state. She formed as clear a mental picture of Candice as she could and began the incantation.

"Crimson candles, burning bright,
Your golden flame a beacon in the night.
Search for a love that's pure and true.
This is all I ask of you.
Lead him haste to Candice's side
And have him ever there abide."

She opened her eyes. The candlelight made everything look perfect— mystical, even——and as the candles burned, the room filled with the scent of honeyed cinnamon.

She'd done it. Successfully performed both spells. Now she only had to sit back and wait for the magic to happen.

NICK DROVE AWAY from Maggie's place, absolutely certain that he'd never understand women. Especially the one who'd just sent him packing. But unlike the other women he knew, who were masters at manipulation, he'd thought Maggie was a straight shooter. If she wanted to be kissed, she let him know. If she wanted him to get lost, she let him know that, too. And she had.

He'd gone to Maggie's place tonight with certain expectations. Such as spending some serious quality time with her. Just the two of them. Alone.

Who was he kidding? He'd expected to make out with her and he had a condom in his pocket to prove it. It made him feel like he was sixteen again, and that wasn't a good feeling.

Face it, Durrance. When it comes to women, you're as dumb now as you were in high school.

He hadn't bought Maggie's excuse about being tired. If anything, she'd looked as gorgeous and bouncy as ever. In the past week and a half, he'd noticed that she had a tendency to babble when she was trying to hide something. Tonight she'd had something to hide, no question about it.

Maybe she had a date.

Not that it was any of his business, but whatever was going on, it annoyed him that she'd openly flirt with him when the spirit moved her and run him out of the house when it didn't.

Who needed it?

Not him, that's for sure. When he saw her tomorrow, he'd make damn sure he wasn't wearing his heart on his sleeve.

Chapter Ten

Maggie woke the next morning feeling triumphant. She stretched her arms over her head and arched her back against the soft cotton sheet. In spite of Gabriella's reservations, the love spells had gone off without a hitch. And even though it was the weekend, Nick was coming to the house to install the soaker tub.

Life was good, and hiring Nick had been one of the smartest moves she'd ever made. He was great at what he did and always seemed to know exactly what she wanted, even when she sometimes didn't. Best of all, they'd become friends. If she hadn't been so preoccupied with Allison's problems all week, she might have tried to get Nick alone to find out just how far beyond friendship they might be able to take their relationship.

They'd have plenty of time for that, though. Starting today.

She jumped out of bed and headed downstairs. She had plenty to do before he got here.

By midmorning, she had tidied up the kitchen, put away the yearbook and candle holders and had two pans of chocolate chip cookies ready to slide into the oven. She'd discovered that Nick liked them warm, and today she was going to make sure he got exactly what he wanted.

Within reason, of course. She wasn't going to rush into anything, especially not Nick's bed, but the possibility still made her smile.

She went out to the front porch when she heard the truck pull up and was a tad disappointed to see that Nick had brought Brent with him. Then she noticed the size of the tub on the back of the flatbed. No way would he be able to maneuver that monster into the house on his own.

Nick barely shot her a passing glance as he stepped out of the truck, then without so much as a "Hey, how's it going?" he started unfastening the ropes that held her tub in place.

Brent, on the other hand, was his usual exuberant self. "G'morning, Maggie. You're looking gorgeous today."

"I'll bet you use that line on every woman you meet."

"Only the gorgeous ones."

She thought she detected a hint of annoyance in Nick's eyes before he turned away. What was his problem?

A person doesn't have to be a rocket scientist to figure that out.

"Do you know something I don't know?" Maggie asked under her breath, wishing Aunt Margaret would stop popping up so unexpectedly.

Plenty. But you'll figure it out. Maybe even before it's too late.

Brent took the front steps two at a time. "I have to take the front door off the hinges."

"Are you sure that thing will fit through here?"

"Yep. We measured."

He stepped inside and tested the air. "Apple pie?"

"No." Why would he ask something like that.

He sniffed again. "Cinnamon buns?"

"N-o-o-o." Hmm. It must be the scent from the candles she'd burned last night. "I was experimenting with…a new hand soap."

His disappointment made her smile. "I have cookies ready to go in the oven and lemonade. And you're both welcome to stay for lunch."

Nick appeared in the doorway behind him.

Brent's eyes lit up, but Nick was shaking his head. "Thanks, but it's been a long week and I have some stuff to do at the office."

Excuse me? The way he mimicked the excuse she'd used last night couldn't be more obvious.

Brent's eyebrows shot up. "What kind of stuff?"

"Just stuff."

Not in a million years would she have expected him to say anything so childish. How dare he be miffed that she'd had other plans last night? It wasn't as if she had to account for her time.

He never asked you to.

Technically, Aunt Margaret was right. All he'd done was come by to measure the bathroom and—

Oh, Maggie. Duh.

Nick hadn't needed to measure the bathroom, at all. He'd already measured it at least a hundred times. She'd never met anyone more meticulous. He'd only used that as an excuse to come back here last night because he wanted to see her. How could she have been so dense?

Not to mention single-minded and stubborn und—

"Not now, Aunt Margaret."

It didn't take them long to get the tub in place, and Nick ignored her the entire time. She hated that he was annoyed with her. They had become friends and he trusted her, all of which were critical for his makeover to be a success. She wanted to apologize, but he wouldn't want her to say anything in front of Brent. She'd have to wait until they were alone. All she had to do was to figure out how to make that happen.

AFTER NICK AND BRENT LEFT, Maggie was at loose ends. She could work on her new tropical delight facial mask, but she felt too restless to concentrate. There was also the brochure she was creating to advertise the opening of the spa, but she couldn't focus on that, either.

She didn't think she'd caused a major setback with Nick's make-over, at least she hoped not. Allison had needed help, and Maggie loved to help people, but Nick should have been her priority. Her conscience niggled at her some more and she made a decision. Between now and Leslie's wedding, she would focus on him. By the time he walked his sister down the aisle, he'd be a new man.

She gazed out the kitchen window. The back garden looked peaceful and inviting, just the kind of solitude she needed right now. She'd go sit out there and devise a plan to get Nick to come back to the house, without Brent, so she could apologize. She'd had plenty of experience with apologies, after all. How many times had she rushed into something, created a problem and had to make things right again?

More times than she cared to think about, but the good thing was that she always learned from her mistakes and, in the end, everything always worked out for the best. A person just had to have faith in what they were doing, and she did. She poured herself a tall frosty glass of lemonade, carried it out to the garden and settled herself into an old wooden lawn chair under the apple tree.

She'd lived her whole life in Manhattan and had always been delighted just to have a few potted plants on the fire escape. On her many trips to visit Aunt Margaret, she'd loved sitting out here. It had never occurred to her, though, that someday this might be hers.

"Thank you, Aunt Margaret."

Nothing. Just as well. She needed time to think. She sipped the lemonade and was deep in thought when she became aware of voices and the sound of hammering coming from Allison's backyard. Her neighbor hadn't mentioned they were having any work done, but it sounded as though they'd hired someone.

She leaned back in her chair and listened more intently. John and Allison were having a discussion but she couldn't make out what they were saying. From the sound of things, their two children were running around the yard having a discussion of their own, at the top of their lungs.

"It's gonna be *my* tree house."

"Isn't."

"Is, too. Girls don't have tree houses."

"Do, too."

A tree house? Now that was interesting. When she'd mentioned it earlier in the week, Allison had all but dismissed the idea. Now, less than twenty-four hours after she'd cast the love spell for her neighbors, they were having a tree house built.

Maggie got up from her chair and casually strolled toward the fence, then followed it until she found a good-sized knothole.

They weren't having a tree house built, they were building it themselves! A pile of lumber had been stacked under the giant oak tree. While their children raced around the lawn, Allison and John studied a sheaf of pages they were holding. They both wore jeans and T-shirts and John had even strapped on a tool belt.

Maggie had never seen him in anything but lawyerly business clothes, but this…this was a different man. Masculine, in spite of the slightly receding hairline, and even a little rugged-looking. Judging by the way Allison was eyeing him, she thought so, too.

Then John put an arm around his wife and patted her on the butt.

Maggie grinned. "Mission accomplished! Am I good, or what?" She did a little dance around her backyard, expecting Aunt Margaret to chime in with a witty comeback, but for once there was no comment. Just as well, she thought, because really, what was there to say?

She settled into her lawn chair, now confident that the spell she'd cast for Candice would be just as effective. With Candice out of the picture, Allison and John could work on rebuilding their relationship. And with Allison's marriage back on track,

Maggie could focus her full attention on Nick. What she needed to do now was to figure out a way to get him back here.

I always heard the best way to a man's heart is through his stomach.

Maggie considered that. Aunt Margaret could be right.

Dinner, she decided, would be the best option. But if she called and invited him, would he come?

NICK SPENT TWENTY minutes channel surfing before turning off the TV in frustration. Most people had a life. That's why there was never anything good on Saturday afternoon. His lame excuse about having stuff to do had prevented him from spending the afternoon with Maggie. If he hadn't let his stupid pride get the better of him, he easily could have figured out a way to get rid of Brent. By now he and Maggie would be—

The phone rang.

He reached for it without thinking. "Hello?"

"Nick? Hi." The rich sound of Maggie's voice sent a thrill through him.

"Hi."

"Hi," she said again. "I, um, I hate to have to tell you this, but—"

"Is everything all right?"

"Well, not really. I think maybe there's going to be a problem with the ceiling."

"The ceiling?"

"Yes. A few chunks of plaster fell down this afternoon."

"Which ceiling?"

"Um, the living room."

That was weird. "Are you sure?"

"I'm sure."

"Okay. I'll be right over to take a look."

"Thanks. I really appreciate it."

"Maggie?"

"Yes?"

"Stay out of that part of the house till I get there, okay?" He couldn't think of anything that could cause the ceiling to collapse, but he didn't want her getting hurt.

"Oh. Sure. How long do you think it'll take you to get here?"

"Give me twenty minutes."

It only took him twelve.

Maggie and the scent of warm chocolate-chip cookies greeted him at the door. She was wearing a sleeveless yellow top, a dark blue knee-length skirt and a strappy pair of sandals to match. Her gorgeous dark red hair had been twisted loosely on top of her head, minus the pencil, and she was wearing her aunt's pearls.

Aside from the shoes, which were just about the sexiest pair of footwear he'd ever seen, it was a combination that would look sensible and demure on any other woman. Especially combined with the aroma of freshly baked cookies. But in spite of the pearls and the cookies, she was the most unconventional woman he'd ever met.

He hadn't seen the pearls since that first day and he couldn't help wondering if she had plans to go out. Maybe even a date. Maybe that's why she'd given him the brush-off last night.

"You look nice," he said.

"So do you. Would you like some cookies and lemonade?"

"I think I'd better take a look at the living room first."

"Right. About that. Um, it might not be as bad I thought."

"Why don't you let me be the judge of that."

She put a hand over her mouth, as though she was trying to hide something, a smile maybe, and looked down at the floor as she cleared her throat.

"There's kind of nothing to look at," she said finally. "I made it up. The story about the plaster falling."

"Why would you do something like that?" And this had better be good, he thought.

"I really did have things to do last night and I needed to be alone. But I didn't realize until this morning that you thought I'd been rude and that you were mad at me, and then Brent was here so I didn't want to apologize, in case you didn't want him to know you'd come here last night and—"

"Maggie?"

Her gaze met his. "Yes?"

"Is there a point to this?"

She nodded. "I wanted you to come over here so I could say I'm sorry."

"You made up a crazy story about plaster falling from the ceiling just to get me over here?"

Her eyelashes fluttered. "It worked, didn't it?"

"It did." He took her chin in his hand and tilted her face to one side, then the other. "But look at the effect it's had."

Her eyes went wide. "What do you mean?"

"I'd say your nose is at least a quarter of an inch longer. Maybe more. In fact," he said, leaning a little closer. "I think it's still growing."

She smiled. "It was just a teensy little fib."

A stray stand of hair dangled from the mass that was pinned loosely against her head, and it was all he could do to resist tucking it into place. "Lucky for you it was just a little one, or this nose might not be looking so gorgeous right now."

That made her laugh. God, he loved the sound of it. If she were part of his life, he'd go out of his way every single day to make her laugh, simply because listening to it made him feel so good. He bent and kissed the tip of her nose. "Smells like those cookies are ready to come out of the oven."

"Not till the timer goes."

She'd no sooner said it than the timer buzzed.

He grinned. "I have kind of a sixth sense about these things."

"Are you making fun of me?"

The hair was finally too much. He caught the loose strand and tucked into place. "I never joke about food."

"I guess Aunt Margaret was right."

Discussions about her aunt always made him wary, mostly because he was never sure if she was referring to the past, or to something Miss Meadowcroft had said…recently. Allegedly said, he corrected. He certainly didn't believe in this supernatural stuff, no matter how endearing it was that Maggie did.

He followed her into the kitchen and tried his best not to hover around the stove. Still, when she opened the oven door and a hot rush of melted chocolate filled the room, he couldn't stop himself from moving in. As she stood at the counter, carefully shifting the cookies onto a rack, he moved up behind her and reached an arm around her, pretending to grab for a cookie but really only wanting her.

"Careful, or you'll get burned."

He had no doubt that was true, in every sense. Falling for Maggie Meadowcroft would be one of the craziest things he'd ever done. He was a practical man. Down to earth. And she was… Then again, neither one of them seemed to fit the mold of Collingwood Station. And two misfits didn't make a right. Did they?

"I'll take my chances," he said. As soon as she set the cookie sheet and spatula on the counter, he turned her around to face him and she stepped readily into his arms. He waited for his better judgment to start in on him, but for some reason it stayed silent.

From the moment he'd first seen her, he'd been mesmerized by her soft brown eyes, but how was it that until now he'd never noticed the little gold flecks in them? He ran his hands down her arms and let them settle at her waist. Everything about her was perfect. The way she smiled, the way she laughed, the way her slender body felt in his hands, even her...

"Cookie?" she said, sliding the warm, gooey treat between his lips before they managed to descend on hers.

He backed off a little and took a bite. "I thought you'd never ask."

"Let's take a plateful and some lemonade out to the garden."

"That's probably a good idea." Given that his idea was a lot less good. Bad, in fact. He picked up the tray and nodded toward the back door. "After you."

He noticed the hammering right away. "What's going on over there?" he asked.

"Allison and John are building a tree house for their kids. Isn't that wonderful?"

Of course. He'd completely forgotten that John had talked to him about it earlier in the week. "Yeah, it's great."

Maggie beamed. "It was my idea, you know."

"I thought it might have been." He would have told her about John's midweek visit, when he'd come over to ask for advice, but she was talking again.

"I knew a tree house would be a lot of fun for the kids. I mean, I grew up in the city where a kid couldn't even dream about having a tree house. But I thought it would be good for Allison and John, too. You know, to have a family project they could all work on together."

Nick nodded. Not that he had any experience with family projects. Dinner was about the only thing the Durrance family had ever done together, and his mother had seen to it that the evening meal was a well-orchestrated event. Other than that, he and Leslie had either received terse orders from their father or long, tedious lectures from their mother.

Nothing about his family constituted a project. A piece of work maybe, but never a project.

"Do you think we should go over to see how they're doing?"

Maggie asked. "I mean, I don't want to intrude, but I'm dying to know what they're building."

Nick was torn. Staying here with Maggie, alone, had a lot of appeal. She'd tricked him into coming over here and he wasn't sure what she'd had in mind, but he'd already come to the conclusion it wasn't sex. She'd gone out of her way to look gorgeous, and she was already one of those women who looked good, no matter what she was wearing. Still, he kept picturing her with nothing on but the shoes and the pearls.

Which meant going next door, before he made a complete ass of himself, was a good idea. Besides, it would also gave him a chance to show that he was better at something than John was.

Petty? Maybe.

Childish? Damn straight.

Did he care? No way.

"Sure," he said. "And if looks like they need a hand, we can offer to help. Otherwise we can leave them to it."

"Good idea. It'll only take me a minute to change," she said. "And we can take the cookies and lemonade with us. The kids might like a snack."

Nick snagged a couple of cookies from the pile before Maggie whisked them away. "Hey, they won't last long once the kids attack them," he said.

She smiled. "Like I told you. They're irresistible."

Nick sat on a lawn chair and munched the cookies while he waited for Maggie. The sounds of hammering and sawing coming from next door were interspersed with laughter and an occasional shriek from one of the children. Maggie's backyard was less formal than Allison's and he had no trouble picturing a couple of kids playing in it. A dreamy-eyed wisp of a girl who had Maggie's spirit and stunning red hair, and a dark-haired adventurous little boy who reminded him of...

"I'm ready." Maggie's reappearance spared him from considering the identity of the father of her as-yet nonexistent children. She was wearing a pair of jeans and an oversized T-shirt that should have had the opposite effect from the outfit she'd just taken off, but it didn't. *Face it,* he told himself. *She looks hot, no matter what she's wearing.*

She sat on the chair next to him, slipped on a pair sneakers and tied them up. "Ready?"

Oh, yeah, he was ready.

NICK WOULD HAVE GIVEN a lot to have a camera when they let themselves through the back gate. Pieces of lumber of various lengths were strewn around the yard and it looked as though John was building a door. A door to what was anybody's guess, since nothing had actually been nailed to the tree.

"Are you sure it's a tree house?" he said quietly to Maggie.

"Positive. Hello!" she called. "Anyone want cookies and lemonade?"

The children raced toward her.

"I do!"

"Me, too!"

Allison called to them from across the yard. "Michael! Meredith! Where are your manners?"

"I do, please!"

"Me, too, please!"

"Me first."

"Me first, too. Please!"

Maggie deposited the plate of cookies on a patio table and scooped the little girl into her arms. "There's plenty for everyone."

Nick set the frosty pitcher and a stack of plastic glasses next to the plate.

Allison walked toward them, smiling. "Maggie, this was so thoughtful of you. Thanks."

Maggie and Allison gave each other a hug, briefly sandwiching a shrieking little girl between them. "It sounded like you guys are hard at work, so I figured cookies and lemonade would hit the spot."

Interesting, Nick thought. Allison's reaction to Maggie's generosity was the polar opposite to what it had been at the barbecue. And that wasn't the only thing that was different. She actually looked normal for a change, in spite of the carefully chosen denim pants, cropped just below the knee and the sleeveless white shirt with the little designer logo on the pocket. She wasn't wearing much makeup, if any, and her hair hadn't been shellacked into place. He glanced at John, who seemed to be having a little trouble keeping his eyes off his wife.

It's about time, Nick thought. Although it was hard to believe that simply building a tree house could bring about a transformation like this, he wasn't about to argue with fate or whatever it was that had caused the guy to finally get his priorities straight.

Maggie settled into a deck chair with the little girl in her lap. The child eyed him suspiciously. "Who's he?"

"This is Nick," Allison said quickly. "He's a friend of Mommy and Daddy's and he's Leslie's brother. He's going to be at her wedding."

"How come I've never seen him b'fore?"

Allison looked uncomfortable. "Nick works really hard, sweetie. He's busy all the time."

"Like Daddy?" Her innocent blue gaze caught Nick completely off guard.

"Kind of." Allison filled one of the glasses with lemonade. "I'm just going to run this over to your dad, okay?"

Nick thought the child might want to run after her mother, but she seemed completely content to stay in Maggie's arms.

"Are you and Maggie going to get married?" she asked.

Nick's throat closed up. Even if he had an answer, he couldn't have coughed it up if his life depended on it.

Maggie—bless her—was never at a loss for words. "Nick and I are just friends." She glanced at him and winked. "Meredith is especially interested in weddings these days because she's going to be Leslie's flower girl."

"I get to carry a basket of flowers," she said with an air of importance that reminded Nick of that old saying about the apple not falling far from the tree.

"That's nice," he said.

"Do you work with my daddy?"

Nick shook his head. "No, I'm just a—"

Maggie interrupted. "You know how your daddy is a lawyer and he fixes people's problems?"

The child gave a solemn nod.

"Well, Nick sort of does the same thing. When he goes to work, he fixes houses so they don't get old and rickety and fall down."

Yeah, Nick thought. *Those are the same, all right.*

But the little girl's head bobbed up and down as though she understood exactly what Maggie was saying. "Is he fixing your house?"

Maggie nodded. "Yes, he is. And when it's finished I'm going to have a housewarming party and you're invited."

"I went to Daddy's office once."

"Was it fun?"

Nick was impressed with Maggie's easy rapport with the little girl, who was shaking her head. "I had to be quiet and I wasn't s'posed to touch anything."

"When you come to my house, you can touch anything you want," Maggie said. "I'll even give you a makeover."

"What's that?"

"You get a facial and some new makeup that makes you look good on the outside, but my makeovers also make you feel good on the inside."

Meredith smiled. "I want to feel good on the inside. Can Mommy have a makeover, too?"

Maggie laughed, but Nick sensed that she was avoiding eye contact with him. "You and your mom can have a mother-daughter makeover. How does that sound?" She tickled the little girl's tummy and made her laugh.

"Good," she said between giggles. "You should give everybody a makeover."

Nick guessed that whatever Maggie whispered in the child's ear was in complete agreement. Considering some of the people he knew in Collingwood Station, she had her work cut out for her. Come to think of it, though, Allison had been a total pain in the butt a week ago. Today she seemed like a different person. More natural and a lot more relaxed, and he had a hunch those changes had a lot to do with Maggie.

How did she do it? She didn't meddle and she didn't tell people what they should or shouldn't do, but if they spent enough time with her, they seemed to figure it out on their own.

Allison and John walked toward them, arms linked.

Meredith wriggled out Maggie's arms and ran toward her father. "Daddy, Daddy, horsey ride!"

John picked up his daughter and set her on his shoulders.

The little girl hooked her hands under her father's chin and tried to lean over his head, presumably to make eye contact while she talked to him. "Nick's coming to the wedding and Maggie's going to give me and Mommy a makeover."

John didn't seem to mind that the fingers clutching his neck were smeared with cookie crumbs and melted chocolate "I guess that means my gorgeous girls will be more gorgeous than ever."

Somehow Nick hadn't pictured John as such an easygoing parent. "How's the project?" he asked.

Nick caught Allison's little eye roll as she turned away from her husband and poured herself a glass of lemonade. "I love the plan we picked out but I think it's going to be a little more challenging than we expected." She was smiling when she turned back to John. "Isn't it, darling?"

"You could say that."

"If you'd like some help getting started, I'm happy to pitch in," Nick said. "Are those the plans?"

John nodded and handed him a sheaf of papers that had been stapled in one corner.

Holy smokes. No wonder the poor guy looked so discouraged. "This is very...ambitious. Doable, though," he said quickly, when he noticed John's worried expression. "And the kids'll have a blast with this."

As he flipped through the pages John had handed to him, most of the smugness he'd felt before coming over here had evaporated. Even if John couldn't build a tree house, he was one helluva lucky guy. He had money, a high-powered career and a great family that clearly adored him. Just not a lot of common sense.

They'd chosen a plan for a tree house that had a shingled roof, shuttered windows and even a deck with a little railing. He scanned the data sheet. Jeez, the place had a hundred square feet. In some parts of the world, people probably raised families in houses less substantial.

Considering his own upbringing, he was being a bit judgmental. Besides, he could see where they were coming from. They had two great kids and if he were ever lucky enough to be in their position, he'd want the best for them, too. Just not the way his parents had done it. All the material stuff in the world didn't make up for disinterest and a complete lack of love and affection. John seemed to be doing a good job of providing everything.

"Where'd you get the plans?" he asked.

"Allison found them on the Internet. She wanted something that would be safe for the kids but not damage the tree."

"Then I'd say this is perfect. And it's good that the plans are so detailed." Nick did his best to hide his amusement as he flipped through to the end. Yes, very detailed. All forty pages. No wonder John seemed so overwhelmed. "Lots of work though."

"Yeah."

"If you'd like a hand—"

Maggie appeared at his side and hooked her arm through his. "We probably can't stay too long. We should get back to my place and finish the, ah, painting. Right?"

Painting? What was she talking about? Nick opened his mouth and closed it again. This was her way of letting him know they should let Allison and John work through this on their own, as a couple. And, of course, she was right.

"I can help you get the anchor bolts and crossbraces in place," Nick said. "That's probably the trickiest part. The rest looks pretty straightforward."

Half an hour later, the supports for the tree house were in place. John walked with him back to the table where Maggie sat with Allison and the kids. "Thanks. This was a big help."

"No problem. It's pretty much what I do for a living, so it's no big deal."

"I don't know about that," John said. "Must be pretty rewarding to be able to look back at the end of the day and see everything you've accomplished."

"Yeah, I guess it is."

"So, I'll probably see you next weekend at Gerald's bachelor party?"

"Wouldn't miss it," Nick lied. Unless he had to have an emergency appendectomy or something.

A guy could always hope.

Chapter Eleven

"That was fun," Maggie said as she and Nick carried the dishes into her kitchen. "And it's good to see Allison and John getting along so well."

Nick gave her an odd look. "Were they having problems?"

Oops. She should have chosen her words more carefully. She'd promised Allison she wouldn't say anything about the situation between her and John. "I just meant that it's great to see married couples that get along." *Like we would,* she thought.

"I see." He didn't look altogether convinced, but at least he seemed willing to drop the subject. "I should probably get going."

She was glad she'd figured out a way to get him to come over that afternoon. They were back on friendly terms again and she intended to keep it that way. In fact, everything was working out perfectly.

Nick was involved with his family again.

The spell for Allison and John had literally worked overnight.

Nick and John were getting along very well. So well that Maggie suspected they'd become friends again. Not like his and Brent's friendship, but friends.

Face it, Maggie. You are good.

"So, you're going to Gerald's bachelor party next week-end?" she asked.

"Looks that way."

Maggie walked with him to the front door. "It sounds like fun."

"About as much fun as a trip to the dentist."

"You never know. Maybe a naked woman will jump out of a giant cake and have her way with the groom."

Nick laughed. "Yeah, I live for stuff like that. But since the groom is marrying my sister, that better not happen."

Maggie liked seeing Nick in overprotective big-brother mode. He cared a lot more about his family than he wanted to let on. "Is Leslie having a bachelorette party?"

"I'm pretty sure it's a bridal shower. My mother wouldn't attend anything as scandalous as bachelorette party. Weren't you invited?"

"No. I've only met your sister once, at the barbecue, so there's no reason I should have been. But if that party was anything to go by, Leslie chose the perfect person to be her maid of honor. I'm sure the shower will be wonderful." In fact, if she was ever in need of a maid of honor, maybe she'd ask Allison.

"I'm pretty sure my mother is organizing it, which means the only thing Allison has to do is show up and do what she's told."

"Your mother sounds formidable."

"Only when she's organizing something or meddling in somebody else's business. Which is pretty much all the time so, yeah, she's formidable."

"I'm sure she means well."

Nick's laugh had no mirth in it. "Let me know if you still feel that way after you've met her."

Time to drop that subject, Maggie decided. It didn't do any good to dwell on how much he and his mother didn't get along. She leaned against the wall, just inside the front door. "So, see you on Monday?"

"Definitely. What are your plans for the rest of the afternoon?" he asked.

Now that the spells were out of the way and she'd patched things up with Nick, she finally had time to focus on her business. "I want to work on some new products for the spa. What about you?"

Nick hooked his thumb into the pocket of his jeans and placed his other hand on the wall above her shoulder, bracing his body close to hers. "I have a few things in mind."

"Oh." She liked the way his closeness made her feel so secure.

"So, I'll see you on Monday."

"Mmm-hmm."

"Unless there's a real plaster disaster and you need me here sooner."

She also loved that he could make her laugh. "I don't think there'll be a disaster."

"But you never know." He inched closer.

"No. You never do." She felt a little breathless.

He gave her a quick, light kiss. "That's what I wanted to do last night."

"I know."

He kissed her again and this time his lips lingered a little longer. "But you were too busy."

"Yes, I was." But she wasn't busy now. Now they were on exactly the same page and the book was about to get very interesting.

He must have been able to read that in her eyes because his next kiss was different. He still leaned against the wall, with only his mouth on hers, yet she heated up as though his body was pressed against hers.

"So what were you doing last night that was more important than this?"

She opened her eyes and tried to focus. "It's a secret."

He withdrew a little and gave her one of his intense looks.

She snagged the front of his shirt with both hands and pulled him back in. "It's a good secret. When the time is right, I'll tell you all about it."

He seemed to relax a little. "Promise?"

"Promise."

"Then I'll just have to be patient, won't I?" His hand wasn't on the wall anymore. It was stroking the side of her head and doing magical, shivery things to that tender spot just behind her ear. This time his kiss had way more urgency and a lot less finesse.

"You're making it very difficult for me to leave," he said finally.

"You're making it hard to let you go."

He touched his forehead to hers. "Do you have any idea what's going on here?"

"Yes. You just kissed me."

"I meant with us."

"I know what you meant." But how was she supposed to answer that question? By saying, 'I think I might be falling in love with you'? How fast would he run if she made that confession? "I'm not sure what's going on. Maybe we shouldn't try to analyze it."

"Maybe not." He kissed her again. Lightly, playfully. "I try to have a strict policy about mixing business with—"

Monkey business?

Before she could stop herself, Maggie pushed him away. *Aunt Margaret? Not now!*

"Something wrong?" he asked.

"No. But I think you're right. Mixing business and…" She paused while she cast a hasty glance around the front hall. "Mixing business and *monkey business* is never a good idea."

He tipped his head back and laughed. "You reminded me of your aunt just then. She used to get after me and Brent all the time. 'Gentlemen, I've had enough of your monkey business,' she used to tell us. Can't say I blame her, either. We were a couple of bad a—"

Maggie quickly covered his mouth with her hand. "I wouldn't say that word if I were you."

Nick's eyes went narrow and he gave her a long, questioning look. "O-kay. You expect me to believe she's here? Right now?"

"Well…"

"Come on, Maggie. You can't be serious."

"Oh, Nick, this is not a good time to question these things."

He gave the ceiling a long, deliberate look. Then he glanced over one shoulder, then the other. "Fine. You've convinced me. She's here." His mouth arched into a mischievous grin. "So, Miss Meadowcroft, how's this for monkey business?"

Before Maggie could stop him, he pulled her into a full-body embrace. His tongue dipped into her mouth, demanding an intimate response and getting it. The kiss alone would have shocked even the most broad-minded spinster aunt, so who knew what she thought when a pair of big, strong hands slid into the pockets on the back of Maggie's jeans.

He ended the kiss and looked down at her, his eyes smoked with passion, but there was still no mistaking the humor. "If I'm being sent to the detention hall, I'm damn well going to make it worth my while. Nobody knows that better than your aunt."

And then he was gone.

"Aunt Margaret?" Maggie asked shakily, after she closed the door. "Are you still here?"

Her question was answered by her aunt's deep, rich chuckle. *I always liked that boy.*

Maggie waited for the "but" that was almost certainly attached to that comment, only it never came.

"Aunt Margaret?"

But it seemed she was gone, too.

Now that's interesting, Maggie thought. Her aunt approved of Nick. What if there was there a chance that he had real feelings for her? More real than just wanting to make out every time they were alone? There was no denying what she felt for him. She wished he was still here, with his hands on her butt and his tongue playing tag-you're-it with hers.

Why did she have so much trouble figuring out her own situation when it was so easy to see what other people needed? And why couldn't she just enjoy a casual relationship instead of falling for the wrong guy, again?

NICK DUCKED OUT of the private room at the country club and headed for his truck. He wasn't a big fan of bachelor parties under the best of circumstances and this one had not gone well. He'd arrived late and had been there maybe a half hour when the stripper showed up. John had seemed as uncomfortable as Nick was, but since he was the best man, he was expected to stick it out. It had taken Nick less than fifteen seconds to decide he didn't want to hang around and watch Gerald drool over a woman in black stilettos and a scaled-down maid's uniform.

For the life of him he didn't know what Leslie saw in the guy, but she was capable of making her own decisions. He was already uneasy about seeing Gerald and Candice together at the barbecue. It's not as though he was the only guy she'd been throwing herself at. At first he'd thought John was messing around with her, but after seeing him with his wife last Saturday, he knew that wasn't the case. So he was probably wrong about Gerald, too.

He decided to drive around a bit instead of going home and the next thing he knew, he was on Maggie's street. Should he stop? Why not? He and Maggie were friends, and friends dropped in on each other.

A week had passed since Maggie had invented the plaster disaster. Nick had come to the conclusion, though, that he really needed to keep his hands to himself until this job was finished. Everything was falling into place and if things continued to go well and all the subcontractors showed up when they said they would, he and Brent should be finished in another week.

Which meant that by the time Leslie's wedding rolled around next Saturday, he would no longer be Maggie's contractor.

And she would no longer be his client.

They would just be friends. Or maybe they would be more than friends. In a week, as soon as he finished the work on Maggie's house, he'd know for sure.

One week. Seven days. He could wait that long. Tonight would just be about two people being friends.

Maggie answered the door and to his surprise, she was looking very formal, in a somber sort of way. "Sorry. I should know better than to show up unannounced. You look like you're going out."

"Oh, no, I'm staying in tonight."

In that get-up? She was wearing a long-sleeved, high-necked black dress that ended halfway between her knees and her ankles. The severe-looking garment was offset somewhat by the pearls and by her hair, which hung loose around her shoulders instead of being wound up and pinned at the back of her head the way she normally wore it. He'd never seen her hair down, and he liked it. A lot.

The dress was another matter. The dress was godawful.

"Are you expecting someone?" He wondered who that might be and felt a little stab of jealousy. "I should have called first."

"No, I'm not expecting anyone but I'm glad you're here. I brought Aunt Margaret's ashes home from the crematorium this week and I was just going to have a little ceremony in her honor. You're just in time to join me."

She stepped aside and waited.

A ceremony for Miss Meadowcroft's ashes? He should have stayed at the bachelor party.

"A ceremony sounds interesting." *Not.* "What do you have in mind?" If she said séance, he was out of here. It was one thing to pay his respects to his old high-school English teacher. Conjuring up her spirit when he'd really hoped to make out with her niece was something else again. Miss Meadowcroft would see right through him.

"Actually, I'm glad you're here. Do you know how to make a gin gimlet?" Maggie asked.

"What?"

"A gin gimlet. It was Aunt Margaret's favorite drink. I thought it would be good to drink a toast to her. She'd like that. And she liked gin gimlets, so that seems to be the obvious choice, don't you think?"

Nick was pretty sure she wouldn't want to know what he was thinking. "If I remember correctly, it's just gin and sweetened lime juice."

"Oooh. I think you're right. There's a bottle of lime cordial in the fridge. I'll bet that's what she used it for." She grabbed his hand and he liked the firmness of her hold on him. "There was a bottle of gin in the sideboard. I put it away in the kitchen before I moved the furniture upstairs."

He allowed himself to be led down the hallway. What the hell, he'd come this far.

She climbed up on a step stool and handed him the gin from the top shelf of a cupboard.

He set the bottle on the counter. "Do you have a cocktail shaker?" he asked.

"Aunt Margaret had one. It's here someplace." Maggie stood on her toes and moved things around in the cupboard. For the first time he noticed the black seam running up the back of her stockings. Holy cow!

The stool wobbled as she leaned to reach the next cupboard. Nick stepped closer, ready to catch her if she fell, but the desire to place the pad of his thumb against the seam and follow it up her leg was almost more than he could resist. How ironic was it that the stockings that had seemed so trashy on the stripper took on a whole different look when teamed up with a dowdy old black dress that smelled faintly of... mothballs?

"Here it is!" She smiled down at him and passed him an old glass-and-chrome shaker.

He held Maggie's hand as she stepped down off the stool, then he set the cocktail shaker on the counter next to the gin while she retrieved the lime juice and some ice.

"Is this everything you need?" she asked.

"We'll need a couple of glasses."

"Of course." She opened another cupboard. "I have these," she said, holding out two of the tumblers she used for serving lemonade.

"A little big," he said. "Anything smaller?"

Glasses clanked as she moved them around. "Oo-ooh. These look elegant." She produced two martini glasses and put the tumblers back in the cupboard.

Nick filled the shaker with ice and measured equal amounts of gin and lime cordial.

"Where did you learn to make gimlets?" she asked.

"You'd be surprised what a kid can pick up hanging around the bar at one of his mother's countless parties."

Maggie watched closely as he put the top on the shaker and shook it.

"Don't bruise the gin," she warned him.

He stopped shaking. "What?"

"Don't bruise the gin. That's what Aunt Margaret always used to say."

"What does that mean?" he asked.

She grinned. "I have absolutely no idea."

Right. He shook the container more gently, trying to dispel the uneasy feeling that the ghost of Miss Meadowcroft would smack him across the knuckles with her ruler if he dared bruise the gin. He strained the gimlets into the two glasses, handed one to Maggie and picked up the other. The drinks were a revolting shade of green. He suspected they might even glow in the dark.

Maggie took a sip of hers. "Mmm. Very nice. Doesn't taste like there's any alcohol in here at all." She sipped again and licked her lips. "I think I like gin gimlets."

He flashed back to the barbecue.

Alcohol goes straight to my head. I guess you could say I'm a cheap drunk.

This could be good. Or not so good. But it was just one drink, he reminded himself. How much of an effect could that have?

"Did I tell you that people have already started to book appointments at the spa?"

He tasted the drink and tried not to make a face. "I don't think you did, but that's good news."

"I thought so, too. I've been dropping off flyers around town, advertising my grand opening, and the first two days are already booked."

She chattered on about the spa's instant success, pausing now and then to sip her drink.

"Oh, would you look at that," she said. "My glass is empty and I haven't toasted Aunt Margaret yet. You better make some more."

Against his better judgment, Nick mixed another shaker of gimlets and refilled her glass.

"Come on." Maggie took his hand. "I put her ashes on the mantel in the living room. That's where I'll keep her after the renovations are finished."

Once again he followed her, resisting the urge to ask where she planned to keep her in the interim.

Maggie had obviously spent some time clearing away the construction debris and there on the freshly dusted mantel, between two vases filled with pink and white roses, stood a silver urn.

He shuddered. Never in a million years could he have

imagined himself standing in Maggie's living room, gimlet in hand, about to a toast a woman who had seen to it that he'd spent a considerable amount of his adolescence in the detention hall.

But Maggie was in her element. She stood next to him and raised her glass.

He raised his, too.

"To Aunt Margaret. One of the dearest, funniest people in the world."

Nick glanced down at her. Was she serious?

"This will always be your home and you're welcome here anytime. Thank you for giving it to me and sorry for making so many changes right away, but it's going to be beautiful, just wait and see."

Nick shifted his weight from one foot to the other and back again. He stared at the drink in her hand, watching the liquid sway from side to side.

"Thank you for always being there for me. I'll always remember the wonderful times we had together, laughing and telling stories."

Okay, this was just plain weird. He could believe that Miss Meadowcroft had a fondness for gin, but a sense of humor? Who knew?

Maggie wasn't finished. "Thank you for teaching me the importance of believing in myself and having a generous spirit." She reached up and touched her necklace. "Oh, and thank you for the pearls."

She smiled up at Nick.

He ground his teeth together. Do not laugh, he warned himself.

"And most of all, thank you for giving me the opportunity to come to Collingwood Station and open my spa and help all these wonderful people." Then she cast a quick, almost worried glance at him.

What was that all about?

"To Aunt Margaret." She lifted her glass a little higher and touched it to Nick's. Then she sipped some of her drink and he did the same.

"Is there anything you'd like to say?" she asked.

"About what?"

"About Aunt Margaret." The drink sloshed in her glass and she giggled before she took another sip.

Yeah. Could you please get lost while I make a pass at your niece? "No. I think you said it all. Perfectly."

"Thank you." She smiled sweetly over the rim of her glass. "Yum. I really like this. Delicious, but it kind of makes you shiver, doesn't it?"

Too green and way too sweet for his liking, but he took a mouthful and did his best to look as though he enjoyed it. He watched her closely, wondering how long before the gin kicked in and what its effect might be.

Maggie drained the glass, then caught a stray drop with her tongue. "Do you think we should have another?"

"Probably not a good idea. This stuff has a way of sneaking up on you."

She put one hand over her eyes, then quickly pulled it away. "Boo!"

Oh, man. This was not looking good. He set his glass on the mantel, pried hers out of her fingers and set it next to his.

She twirled around. "I'm so glad you knew how to make gim ginlets." That brought on more giggling. "I mean…gin…gim-lets."

Not good at all. "Have you had anything to eat today?"

She tipped her head back in thought and swayed a little. "A fruit salad for lunch."

He reached for her and held her gently by the shoulders. "Dinner?"

She shook her head.

"I think we should find you a place to sit down."

She twirled out of his grasp and lost her balance again. "Oops!"

Maggie settled easily into his arms and leaned against him. If he were to let her go, he wasn't sure she could stand on her own. Cheap drunk didn't even come close to describing her.

He'd managed to get himself into a lot of trouble with Miss Meadowcroft back in high school, and for nothing nearly as bad as getting her niece drunk. So on the very remote chance that there were such things as ghosts, he hoped Maggie's aunt had gone someplace else tonight because he really, really didn't want her to see this.

Maggie gazed up at him and to his complete surprise, she kissed him. A long, slow, sweet kiss that sucked the breath out of him. He tightened his arms around her and held her close. She wound her arms around his neck and slipped her tongue between his lips.

In a perfect world, where gorgeous sexy funny women didn't get hopelessly drunk on a few ounces of gin, he might have more restraint. But, what the hell? He'd wanted to kiss her ever since he'd arrived. And it wasn't as if anything else was going to happen tonight, not while she was in this condition.

He held on to that resolve until her hands, still cool from holding the icy gimlet glass, slid under his shirt and up his chest.

He pretty much lost his mind at that point but that was okay because his hand seemed to have one of its own. He brought her in closer and while one hand searched the back of the dress for a zipper, the other slid slowly up the front. When it met no resistance, it shaped itself to one breast.

There was no zipper in the back of the dress. The fog lifted just long enough for him to remember seeing a row of buttons down the front. Did he dare?

No.

Maggie's tongue swirled against his.

What the hell?

The top button opened easily.

Maggie broke the kiss and smiled dreamily at him. "I forgot to ask if you like my dress."

He blinked. "Yeah." What was not to like? She was in it and if that first button was anything to go by, getting her out of it would be a piece of cake.

"It's one of Aunt Margaret's."

Five little words that felt like a bucket of cold water. What the hell had he been thinking? There'd been no harm in kissing an inebriated woman, but trying to get her out of her dead spinster aunt's dress was a bad idea. Really bad. Especially if the aunt was watching.

THE NEXT MORNING Maggie woke with her tongue stuck to the roof of her mouth and her head stuffed with cotton. She hoisted her head off the pillow and let it fall back. No, make that a ten-pound boulder.

Ugh. How could one drink, especially a drink that tasted so yummy, make her feel so miserable?

No, wait. She'd had two drinks. "Please tell me I didn't have more than two drinks," she said out loud.

You never could hold your liquor. You must get that from your mother's side of the family.

"There's nothing wrong with that,"

Didn't say there was. I was just making an observation.

"Please leave me alone, Aunt Margaret. I'm not in the mood for this." She pulled a pillow over her head to drown out her aunt's laughter.

Memories of how the events of the previous night had unfolded slowly crystalized. She groaned into the pillow. She had literally thrown herself at Nick.

She tossed the pillow aside and quickly assessed her present situation. She was upstairs on her bed, lying on top of the bedspread, still wearing Aunt Margaret's black dress. Had Nick helped her up here? Put her to bed? Covered her with this old afghan?

She groaned again. What must he think of her now? She wished she could remember what they'd talked about but for the life of her, the entire evening—pretty much after that first sip of gin—was a blur. Except the part about trying to seduce Nick.

Oh, Maggie. It looks as though another apology is in order. Good thing you have so much experience with them.

But this time she was in no hurry. The apology could wait until Monday. By then she'd be able to think clearly.

"I don't suppose you can tell me how long a gin gimlet hangover lasts?"

Silence. Not even a chuckle.

Humph. She heaved herself out of bed and tried to remember if she knew any herbal remedies for the aftereffects of overconsumption.

Chapter Twelve

On Monday morning Nick arrived at Maggie's, charged with a sense of anticipation. Paint cans were stacked in a pyramid on the front porch and through the open front door, he could see Brent spreading drop cloths over the newly refinished hardwood floor in the hallway.

Nick unloaded the lumber for the new front steps he was going to build. Yes, sir. If everything went according to plan, they would finish the job by the end of the week. Which meant that by Saturday, he would no longer be working for Maggie.

He would take her to his sister's wedding and make damn sure she didn't drink anything stronger than Kool-Aid. Then he'd figure out some excuse to take her to his place after the reception, far away from Miss Meadowcroft's prying eyes.

Did ghosts have eyes?

Not that he actually believed Maggie's wild idea that her aunt was still hanging around, but *she* believed it. As crazy an idea as that was, he didn't want there to be even a remote suggestion that Miss Meadowcroft's ghost might be watching when they finally—

"G'morning, boss." Brent checked his watch. "Not like you to be this late."

"I was on the phone with the roofing company. I convinced

them to start tomorrow so we can get this place finished by the end of the week."

"Have we got another job lined up?"

"Not yet."

Brent pried the lid off a paint can. "So what's the hurry?"

"Maggie's counting on us to get the job done and I don't want to let her down."

There was no sign of Maggie, though, and he wondered if she was home this morning. He had thought about checking up on her yesterday but decided against it. Most people preferred to nurse a hangover in private, and he'd bet hers had been a doozy.

He smiled to himself. That had been some kiss, and he'd come this close to taking their relationship a step beyond professional. Maybe would have, if Maggie hadn't had too much to drink, and if she hadn't started talking about ghosts and if she hadn't been wearing that hideous dress.

"Maggie's never said anything about the job taking too long." Brent's suggestive smirk was more annoying than usual. "So I think we both know what you want."

Nick ignored him. "You should be able to get the living room painted today, right?" With the counter and new plumbing installed, it wasn't a living room anymore, but he wasn't sure what else to call it. The makeover room? A couple of nights ago it had nearly become the make-out room.

"I can finish it today. Might get the hallway done, too, if you stay out of my way."

Brent gave him an exaggerated wink, then glanced down at the paint can. "What the hell? This is purple. The paint store must have made a mistake."

"It's not a mistake. Maggie wants one wall in each room painted Passionate Purple."

Brent looked up at him and grinned. "Seriously?"

"Would I joke about something like that?"

"Nope. You don't have enough imagination to think that up on your own."

"Thanks."

"What color does she want on the other walls?"

"It's kind of a beige color. I think it's called Vanilla Fudge."

"Vanilla Fudge, huh? Passionate Purple. I'm impressed you know these things."

"Don't be. Maggie told me what she wanted and I ordered it."

"You sure that's all she wants?"

Nick wished Maggie would put in an appearance, if for no other reason than to make Brent behave. "What's up with you this morning? You're even more of a smart-ass than usual."

"You got a problem with that?"

Nick knocked his friend's ball cap askew. "It'd be less of a problem if it was at somebody else's expense."

"Right. I'll just have to pick on Maggie when she shows up."

"You haven't talked to her?"

"No. The front door was locked so I let myself in." Brent grabbed the stepladder that was leaning against the wall and carried it into the living room.

"I see." But he didn't. No matter what kind of crazy concoction she was working on, she always greeted them at the door in the morning. Maybe he should have checked on her yesterday.

"She's here, though. I heard her banging around out in the backyard. If you hadn't shown up by the time I was ready to start painting, I was going to check to see what she wanted me to do and ask her about the things on the mantel. Seems kind of weird, don't you think? That she'd put this stuff up there before we finished painting?"

The flashback to Saturday night caught Nick completely off guard. "Oh, that. It's a memorial to Miss Meadowcroft. I don't think she plans to leave it there."

Brent opened a can of the beige paint and picked up a paint stirrer. "And you know this…how?"

"I dropped by on Saturday night when she was getting it set up."

"You sly dog." Brent tossed the wooden stick in the air, watched it twirl a few times, caught it on its downward spiral and dipped it into the paint. "I thought you were supposed to be at the big bachelor party on Saturday."

"I put in an appearance."

There was more smirking from Brent as he set up the stepladder near the fireplace. "I probably would have done the same thing if I were you."

"Put in an appearance?"

"Blown off Gerald Bedford the Third to spend the evening with a gorgeous woman. In a heartbeat."

Right. And Nick didn't need to ask which woman. "Seems to me you've always had your pick of gorgeous women."

"Yeah, it's a gift," Brent said, but there seemed to be a touch of bitterness in his voice. "But getting back to you and Maggie and Saturday night—"

"I don't have a lot in common with Gerald and his buddies so I stayed for the obligatory drink, listened to a few of their off-color jokes and split." Brent didn't need to know about the stripper. "I was sort of at loose ends so I dropped by to check on a few things."

Brent stirred the Vanilla Fudge, poured some into a paint tray and set it on the stepladder. "And I take it everything checked out?"

Nick had no intention of revealing the details of his close encounter with Maggie, but he also knew Brent wouldn't let up until his curiosity had been satisfied. He nodded in the direction of the fireplace. "She was having a memorial for her aunt. That's who's in the silver urn up there on the mantel."

"It's pewter."

"Give me a break."

"I'm just saying—"

"Fine. The pewter urn."

"And the martini glasses?"

"Maggie wanted to drink a toast to her aunt and asked me to mix some cocktails."

"All right," Brent drawled. "Now we're getting somewhere."

"Not really. She's not much of a drinker so the gin went straight to her head. Then it turned out she was wearing one of her aunt's old dresses, so the whole thing ended up being—" he hesitated, realizing he'd already said too much "—awkward."

Brent laughed. "Since when did you get awkward around a gorgeous woman in any kind of dress?"

Nick felt the color rise in his face. "Like I said, it was her aunt's dress." He lowered his voice a little. "She thinks her aunt is still hanging around here."

"What? You mean, the place is haunted?"

"How would I know? Normal, rational, sane people don't believe in that stuff."

"Well, I wouldn't be too quick to rule it out."

"You're kidding me, right?"

Brent shrugged. "I'm not saying I believe in ghosts, but I'm not saying I don't. Lot's of stuff happens that we can't explain."

Nick let his eyes roll upward. "Not you, too."

"I'd watch what I say, if I were you. If Miss Meadowcroft really is hanging around, she's probably not too happy that you got her niece drunk and tried to seduce her."

"The drinks were Maggie's idea. And we didn't—"

Aw, hell. There was no point in denying that he'd set out to seduce Maggie. Brent would never believe him anyway. And he definitely couldn't tell him that she'd made the first move, or that he'd happily gone along with it till he'd been spooked by the idea of Aunt Margaret's ghost checking out the action.

"You were saying? We didn't...what?"

"Never mind." He jammed both hands into his pockets. This was crazy, damn it. Ghosts didn't exist and while it was kind of endearing that Maggie thought they did, Brent's willing acceptance was just plain annoying. "Much as I'd like to continue this airy-fairy discussion about incurring the wrath of a dead woman, we have work to do."

"Wow. It must have been an interesting evening if it incurred wrath."

"Can we just get to work?"

"Yes, sir." Brent raised a paintbrush in mock salute. "If it's all right with you, I think I'll start with Vanilla Fudge and save the passion for later."

"Passionate Purple."

"Whatever you say, boss."

Brent was really starting to bug him. "Just make sure you follow Maggie's instructions. It has something to do with... I don't know. Some plan for where things go in a room."

"Feng shui?"

"How do you know this stuff?"

"I'm a well-rounded human being."

"Yeah, right." Nick felt like a jerk for being bad-tempered. He didn't give a damn whether or not Brent believed in ghosts, but it honestly bothered him that Maggie did. Everything else about her was pretty much perfect. She was one of the most naturally beautiful women he'd ever seen. Her kisses were passionate and unrestrained. Best of all, she accepted people at face value. She didn't meddle or tell people what she thought they should do, and yet the people around her somehow became better people. He couldn't explain it, but he could even see it in himself. The only problem was her unquestioning belief in all this supernatural mumbo-jumbo.

How was he supposed to deal with ghosts and horoscopes and sixth senses and chop suey for the rest of his life?

"Since you're in such a big hurry to put me to work, how 'bout you move this stuff off the fireplace while I get the rollers out of the truck. Then stay out of my way, because I'll be a lean, mean painting machine."

Nick looked at the urn. "I'll see if I can find Maggie and get her to move it."

But Maggie was nowhere to be found. She wasn't in the kitchen and there was no sign of her in the backyard. Maybe she'd gone upstairs? He had no intention of venturing up there.

Fine, then. Much as he'd rather not have to handle a dead woman's ashes, he'd move the stuff himself.

He carefully picked up the silver—pewter—urn.

The lid rattled.

Damn. He tucked it securely under one arm and picked up the glasses. Both contained gimlet residue and one was rimmed with Maggie's pink lipstick. He took a good, close look at the imprint of her lower lip on the outside of the glass. He'd ended up wearing a little bit of that lipstick, too, but what he remembered most was Maggie's gin-flavored kisses. Yes, it had been quite a night.

He held the urn snugly in the crook of his left arm and curled the fingers of that hand around the stems of the glasses. They clinked together and the lid rattled again.

Who would put ashes in an urn that didn't have a good, secure lid?

With his right hand free, he reached for a vase. It was heavier than he expected. A lot heavier. How much water had Maggie put in that thing?

He took half a step forward to get a better grip on it. The toe of his work boot caught on a fold in the drop cloth and the vase went sideways.

"Damn!" Water and roses cascaded down the front of the fireplace. He took a step back to regain his balance and the drop cloth went with him.

The vase shattered on the hearth.

He staggered sideways, shaking his foot to free it from the drop cloth. By the time his shoulder connected with the stepladder, he'd gained enough momentum that the wobbly structure couldn't withstand the impact.

On his way down, his mind went empty, except for one thought.

Do not drop Miss Meadowcroft.

He released his grip on the glasses, braced the urn against his chest and clamped a hand over the lid.

The paint tray clattered to the floor and he landed on his backside in a puddle of paint. Rose water was streaming across the plastic to meet the paint and there was broken glass everywhere.

Brent rushed into the room and Maggie was right behind him. They both stared, wide-eyed. For a few seconds they looked at him as though he was some kind of moron. Then they burst out laughing.

What the hell? "This is not funny."

Brent clapped his hands together a few times. "Oh, yes, it is," he gasped.

Maggie, doubled over and with tears streaming down her face, seemed incapable of saying anything.

"You okay?" Brent asked her.

She nodded.

"Hello? *I'm* not okay. Could you give me a hand up?" Not for anything was he going to relinquish his grip on Aunt Margaret.

Still laughing, Brent took a few careful steps into the room and offered him a hand. "You think this could be some of that wrath you were talking about?"

"You find this funny? It's going to take us all morning to clean up this mess, which means we'll be behind schedule."

"What do you mean 'us'? You diss the ghost of Miss Meadowcroft and I have to clean up the aftermath? Or should I say, after-wrath?"

"Not funny." Nick crossed the room, doing his best to ignore the crunch of glass under his boots, and handed the urn to Maggie. "At least I didn't drop her," Nick said.

That set them off all over again.

"Fine. Have a good laugh at my expense. I don't know what I said to piss her off this much, but at least she should be glad she's not mixed up with all that water and paint."

Maggie held a hand over her mouth in an unsuccessful attempt to control her laughter.

He brushed by her, but didn't miss the way she angled her head to take a gander at his paint-covered butt.

"I'm going home to change." Their hilarity followed him out the door. That's right people, yuck it up. At least they had to clean up the mess.

MAGGIE CARRIED THE URN into the kitchen and set it on the table.

My goodness, that felt good.

"Excuse me?"

I might be dead but I can still appreciate a good strong pair of arms.

"Aunt Margaret! I'm shocked."

Sure you're not jealous?

"That's the craziest thing I've ever heard."

Don't let him get away, Maggie. He's a good man.

"He is, isn't he? You know, I think I might be— " She hesitated, afraid to say it out loud.

I know. You're in love with him.

"You don't think he's figured it out, do you? I mean, what if he's just being nice because he feels he has to be. What if he's only interested in…you know?"

All men are interested in that. But judging by the way he looks at you, he wants more than sex.

"You really think so?"

I know so.

Maggie gently set the urn on the table. "You'll have to sit here for now till I find another place for you. By the way, that stuff with Nick and the ladder and the paint and everything. You didn't—"

Aunt Margaret's deep, rich laugh seemed to fill the kitchen. *Of course not, dear, but he seemed to think I did.*

"Well, I guess it wouldn't hurt to let him keep on thinking that. For a while, anyway."

I guess it wouldn't.

Maggie had been absolutely certain that Aunt Margaret would never do anything to sabotage the project. Still, having a bad day might be a good thing if it made Nick less skeptical.

"I love you, Aunt Margaret."

I love you, too, dear. Now, don't you have work to do?

Maggie smiled. Yes, she certainly did. The possibility that Nick was becoming a believer called for a special lunch. Mr. Donaldson's pizza. She'd run out and pick up a couple of them right now. While she was at it, she'd take him a sample of her Vitamin E hand cream. Last time she'd been in the deli, she'd noticed that his hands were red and chapped, probably from constant hand-washing and from handling all those cold meats and cheeses all day. Come to think of it, a bar of green-tea soap would be good, too. She wrapped a fresh bar in brown paper, tied it with a piece of raffia and popped it into her bag along with the cream.

"Brent?" she called on her way out the front door.

"Yo?" He staggered out of the living room with a huge roll of paint-covered drop cloths in his arms.

She held the door open for him. "I have a few errands to run. Do you need help with this mess before I leave?"

His eyes brightened. "I'm good. I don't suppose you're stopping by the deli, are you?"

"I might be. Why? Are you already thinking about lunch?"

"I'm always thinking about lunch."

She laughed. "Then you won't be disappointed." Neither would Nick, she hoped.

THE BELL on the deli door jangled when Maggie stepped inside.

"Be right with you," Mr. Donaldson called from the walk-in freezer at the back of the store.

"Maggie?"

She turned around at the sound of her name. Allison, Candice and Leslie were sitting at a small table by the window.

"Hi. Nice to see you." Although things seemed to be working out wonderfully for Allison and John, Maggie was still a little surprised to see her with Candice. Why would she continue to be friendly with a woman she suspected of being after her husband?

Keep your friends close, and your enemies closer.

She'd heard Aunt Margaret say that once and she'd never forgotten it. Not that she had any enemies, but she'd liked the sound of it. And Aunt Margaret was a wise woman, so maybe Allison was doing the smart thing.

"Would you like to join us?" Leslie asked.

"Thanks. I'd love to." It would give her a chance to get to know Leslie a little better before the wedding on Saturday and, with any luck, she'd find out if the spell she'd cast for Candice was working as well as Allison and John's.

Mr. Donaldson appeared behind the counter. "Good morning, Maggie. You here to join the other girls?"

"Hi, Mr. Donaldson. I came to get a pizza for lunch, but Allison and her friends have invited me to join them."

"You still feeding those boys?"

"I am. The house has turned out even better than I'd hoped. Nick thinks this will be their last week, and I hope to open the spa by the end of the month."

"Okay, first order of business. If you're feeding Nick Durrance *and* Brent Border, you're going to need more than one pizza. As for the house, I was by there the other day and it's looking mighty good. Margaret would be pleased."

"Yes, I think she is—would be, that is."

Mr. Donaldson scrutinized her over the top of his bifocals. "So, you're having pizza today instead of sandwiches. Sounds like a party."

"Not really. I just thought it would be nice to change things up a bit. You have them ready to go, don't you? The kind I can put in the oven when I get home?"

"Sure do, but I'll make a couple of fresh ones for you. They'll be ready to go when you are."

"Thanks. I'm not sure what kind to get, though."

"Don't you worry about that. I know exactly what those boys like on their pizza. But first, what can I get you? Herbal tea? Maybe a nice iced coffee?"

"Can you make a nonfat chai latte?"

He chuckled. "I can do it all. Got to keep up with the times, you know. You have a seat. I'll bring it over."

"Thanks, Mr. Donaldson." She turned away from the counter, then remembered she had something for him. "I almost forgot." She dug in her bag and took out the hand cream and the green-tea soap. "These are for you. When I was here the other day, I noticed how rough your hands are. These are completely natural and if you use them for a couple of days, I guarantee all that dry, red skin will heal right up."

He read the ingredients on the jar label, then gave her an exaggerated wink. "Interesting. But folks might think it's kind of strange for an old fella like me to start using beauty products."

She winked back. "Then think of them as health products. Besides, 'folks' don't need to know."

He laughed. "You remind me a lot of your aunt."

"Thank you. I'm going to take that as a compliment."

"I meant it as one. Now you go sit with the rest of the girls and I'll make your latte."

Allison and Leslie had scooted their chairs closer to Candice and pulled in a chair from the next table. The "girls" were drinking cappuccinos. Leslie had a leather-covered notebook open in front of her and a pen in her hand.

"Wedding plans?" Maggie asked.

She smiled. "Yes. And I'm so glad we ran into you. I could use your help with something."

"Really? What's that?"

"Nick."

"Oh." Maggie had expected her to say she wanted a facial or a manicure. "What would you like me to do?"

"He still hasn't gone in for his tuxedo fitting. I've left messages at his apartment, on his cell phone and with his answering service, but he never returns my calls."

Candice was shredding her paper napkin and rolling the pieces into tiny little balls. "I don't see why you're so surprised. I mean, isn't this just so typically Nick? He's been like this since high school."

Maggie might have reacted to that comment, but at that moment the only thing bothering her was the nervous paper shredding. If Aunt Margaret were here, she'd tell the woman to sit up straight and stop fidgeting.

Allison swirled her spoon through the foam on her cappuccino and popped it into her mouth. "He spends all day at Maggie's. You could go over and ask him in person."

Leslie scrunched up her nose. "I know you're keeping Nick busy," she said to Maggie, "but you see him every day, so I was hoping maybe you could—"

Maggie's sixth sense finally engaged. Leslie didn't want to drop by the house to see Nick because she didn't want to see Brent. Interesting.

"No worries. I'll ask Nick to call you." Better yet, maybe she'd figure out a way to accompany him to the tuxedo rental place. While she was there, she could drop off some brochures for her men's spa treatments. And get a preview of Nick in his tuxedo.

Leslie wrote *Maggie* next to Nick's name on her list.

Maggie definitely liked the look of her name paired with his, even if it was someone else's list.

Mr. Donaldson came out from behind the counter with a tray. He set a large latte cup and saucer in front of Maggie and a small plate of biscotti in the middle of the table. "These are on the house."

Leslie reached for one and smiled up at him. "That's so sweet of you. I've been counting calories so my dress will still fit on Saturday, but I do love these."

"I know you do. Enjoy." He turned his attention to Allison. "John tells me you're building a new house."

Allison laughed. "He told you about the tree house? The kids are so excited. They've even talked John into a camp-out when it's finished."

"That sounds like fun," Maggie said.

Leslie agreed. "I wasn't sold on the idea when you first mentioned it, but it does sound great."

Candice didn't say anything, but her Cruella De Vil eyebrows spoke for her.

Seldom had Maggie met anyone she couldn't relate to on some level, but she found it nearly impossible to connect with Candice. She seemed unhappy and self-centered and didn't seem to have a nice thing to say about anyone.

As though Mr. Donaldson had read her thoughts, he winked at her before he turned his attention to Candice. "Nice new car you're driving these days."

She brightened immediately. "You saw it? Isn't it gorgeous? I've always wanted a sports car," she said. "I just picked it up last week. When did you see me?"

"Last night. You had a friend with you."

Something that could be interpreted as panic flashed across the woman's face, but Mr. Donaldson hadn't finished. "Looked to me like you were chauffeuring a gentleman friend."

Aha. Maggie knew for a fact that John had been at home with Allison last night because even after they'd put the kids to bed, she'd heard them working in the yard.

"Now you just need to find a man for Maggie and you'll all be taken care of." Mr. Donaldson glanced at his watch. "My goodness, time for me to get back to work. You girls have a nice chat and let me know if you need anything."

Leslie reached for a second biscotti.

"Careful," Allison warned.

"These are so worth an extra hour on the treadmill."

"I'm sure Gerald will be happy to help you work off a few calories."

Leslie's face went pink. "Sounds like you've been getting your exercise, too. You've actually been working on the tree house thing with John?"

"It's been a lot of fun." Allison looked like the cat that got the cream. "You know I'm not one to kiss-and-tell but things have been…good."

"Go on," Candice said.

"I have Maggie to thank for this. Remember that morning a couple of weeks ago, when you came over and we talked?"

Maggie nodded.

"The tree house was her idea," Allison said to her friends. "When I mentioned it to John, he agreed. We've been working on it with the kids and it's been great. It's turned into this whole big family project and…what can I say? After we get the kids to bed, John and I suddenly have all kinds of grown-up stuff to do."

Yes! Maggie congratulated herself. The spell had worked.

Leslie doodled a little heart with an arrow through it in the margin of her notebook. "I thought you've been looking relaxed lately." She gave everyone at the table a sly look. "Now we know why."

"Enough about me," Allison said. "I'm dying to know who Candice was with last night."

"Nobody important."

Allison scooped more foam from her cappuccino. "Girl, we need details."

"It's not serious," Candice said. "Besides, if it doesn't work out, I'd just as soon not have to talk about it."

"So you're not bringing him to the wedding?" Leslie asked.

Candice appeared to be on the verge of swallowing her tongue.

"Okay, I get it." Allison leaned toward Maggie, one hand to her mouth, and spoke in a stage whisper. "Candice is slumming again." Then she put hand down and laughed. "Last time she had a secret affair, it turned out to be with one of Senator Wainwright's stable boys. She whisked him off to the Bahamas for the weekend and when they came home, the poor fellow got fired *and* dumped, all on the same day."

"Oh, and don't forget the married guy," Leslie said. "We only heard about him after his wife threw all his stuff into the driveway." The she patted Maggie's hand. "Don't look so shocked. This is Collingwood Station. Everyone knows everyone else's business."

Maggie's opinion of Candice sank to a record low, but she knew the love spell would never result in anything so icky. Candice might not be willing to unveil the current man in her life, but Maggie believed in the power of love. Whoever the woman was with, chances were very good that he was the perfect man for her.

Leslie glanced at her watch. "Well, girlfriends, it's been fun but I still have a million things to do." She touched Candice's arm briefly. "You'll let me know if you change your mind and decide to bring your mystery man to the wedding?"

Candice lowered her head and dug through her oversized handbag. Her response was muffled, but Maggie was pretty sure she said, "He already has plans."

Maggie said goodbye and watched them gather up their bags and leave before she went up to the counter.

Mr. Donaldson handed her two pizza boxes. "They're all ready to go."

"How long do I have to cook them?"

"The instructions are right here on the box."

"Thanks." She hesitated, not sure if she should ask him about the new man in Candice's life. She wasn't trying to be nosy. She just wanted to congratulate herself on two successful love spells and call her mother and gloat. Just a little.

"They're nice women, aren't they?"

"I've known them all their lives. Leslie and Allison are good girls, but that friend of theirs has always been a bit of a handful."

Maggie silently congratulated herself on having so quickly worked Candice into the conversation. "Now that she has a new man in her life, do you think maybe she'll settle down and live happily ever after? Like Leslie and Allison?"

Mr. Donaldson quirked an eyebrow. "Not a lot goes on in this town that I don't know about. I don't go in for gossip, but I've got eyes."

"So you're saying you know who he is?"

He gazed over the top of his glasses. "I'm saying it's none of my business."

Maggie hadn't expected that answer. Why would talking about Candice and her new friend be gossip? Unless…

While Maggie walked the two blocks home, she thought back to the night she'd cast the love spells. She'd given Nick the brush-off so she could do the spells. And then she'd spent way too much time looking at his yearbook picture instead of focusing on the task at hand. And she hadn't seen him yesterday. What if she'd somehow messed up the spell and he had gone out with Candice?

That was crazy. Nick didn't even like her.

But her mother had warned her that it was a powerful spell.

I told you no good would come of messing around with things you know nothing about.

"Actually, Aunt Margaret, I don't remember you saying that."

Then I guess you weren't listening.

"This is not helping." She reviewed everything that had been said. Candice had looked extremely guilty at being found out. Maybe her new man was married? No, that didn't make sense. Maggie was sure the spell wouldn't work on someone who was married, or on some poor guy who'd lose his job and have his heart broken.

But what if Candice couldn't take her new man to Leslie's wedding because he already had a date? Allison and Leslie had probably told her that Nick had asked Maggie to be his date for the wedding.

Ugh. Please, please, please don't let it be Nick. How bad would life suck if Candice ended up with the man Maggie had fallen in love with?

ON FRIDAY AFTERNOON Nick loaded the last toolbox into the back of his truck and went inside. It had been a brutal week and Brent had done a fair bit of grumbling about the pace Nick had set for them, but the job was finished.

The past week had been torture and on more than one occasion Nick had been tempted to do something he'd have regretted.

Like Monday afternoon, when Maggie had joined him on her porch and talked his ear off while he'd built her new front steps.

He'd opened up in a way he never had before and afterward he'd been shocked by the things he'd told her, about how he'd never been able to live up to his father's expectations and how insecure his sister's successes had made him feel.

Or Tuesday morning, when she'd decided to help them paint and he'd been unable to resist wiping the purple spatters off that adorable little nose of hers. Or Wednesday, when he'd cut his hand while changing a saw blade and she'd massaged aloe vera lotion onto it. And the list went on. He'd needed every ounce of willpower to be in the same room with her and to keep his hands to himself.

With the work completed, the only thing on his mind was taking his relationship with Maggie to the next level. Ask her out on a proper date, away from the house and far away from any possible encounter with her aunt. He believed that Maggie was simply being visited by her many fond memories of the aunt she loved so much, but there was no convincing her of that. And he didn't care. Not anymore. It was just one of the quirky things that made her so special.

Chapter Thirteen

The morning of the wedding Maggie was still in her bathrobe when she heard the thunk-thunk-thunk of the knocker on the front door. Nick had wanted to fix the doorbell but she had found the perfect brass door knocker at a flea market.

"It's open," she yelled downstairs.

She heard the door open and close.

"Nick? Is that you?"

"Yes, and I think you should keep your door locked and not invite people in until you know who they are."

How sweet was that? "This is Collingwood Station," she called down to him. "And I was expecting you, remember?"

"Are you ready? The wedding starts at ten."

"Yes! I'll be right down," she lied, gazing at her reflection in the mirror. Her makeup looked natural and understated. Her hair was another matter. There were times she wished she was a nice sedate brunette, and this was one of them. She twisted her hair and pinned it up, then pulled out the pins and let it down again.

Up or down?

Up looked a bit schoolmarmish. Down looked too casual.

Face it, Maggie. Stunningly elegant has always been out of reach.

She pinned it up again. Casual was definitely out.

"Maggie? You just about ready?"

She glanced at the clock. "Sorry! I'll be right down." She slipped out of her robe, flung it on the bed and reached for the purple dress hanging on the back of the closet door. She'd fallen in love with it the instant she'd laid eyes on it. The shimmery silk fabric flowed deliciously against her skin and the pearls were perfect with it.

But, best of all, she loved the sequined mauve flats and matching bag she'd found to go with the dress. She slipped her feet into the flats and took one last look in the mirror. Almost as an afterthought, she tucked a lavender-colored silk flower into her hair. There. That was the best she could do and she'd already kept Nick waiting far too long.

She dashed downstairs and came to a breathless halt in her front hall.

Wow!

Some men were born to wear tuxedos, and Nick was one of them. Her imagination had not done him justice. Nick in a tuxedo was...well, unimaginable.

"Sorry it took me so long to get ready," she said.

Judging by his appraisal, the effort had been worth it. "So much for the bride being the most beautiful woman at the wedding."

Was he serious? It was never good to upstage the bride. "Do you think I should change? I can wear that black dress of Aunt Marg—"

"No! We're not going to a funeral. Besides, that was meant to be a compliment. Your dress is perfect, you're perfect and we're late."

"I'm sorry," she said again. Meeting Nick's mother for the first time was part of the problem, even though she'd never tell him that. She never worried about what people thought of her, yet she couldn't shake the feeling that she wouldn't measure up to Lydia Durrance's standards.

While she locked the front door, Nick opened a huge umbrella and held it over her. The rain was falling so hard, it bounced back up off the sidewalk.

"It's really coming down," she said after they were both seated in the black sedan he was driving.

"Yeah. My mother will be ticked." He sounded almost happy about it. "This is a rental, by the way. My mother decided my truck wasn't right for the occasion."

"It goes well with your tuxedo. And rain on your wedding day is a good thing. Very lucky."

He smiled at her as he pulled away from the curb. "Lucky, huh? You see the bright side to everything, don't you?"

She smiled back. "Not everything. For example, I don't think anything positive can come from drinking gin gimlets."

Nick laughed but kept his attention on the street ahead of them. "That was a whole week ago." He increased the speed of the windshield wipers.

"And yet the memory is still so vivid."

"Well, if Maggie Meadowcroft can't find the bright side to a hangover, then there mustn't be one."

She loved their easy conversation. "I learned not to drink gin on an empty stomach. I guess that's something positive."

"So you're saying you'll try another gimlet as long as you've had something to eat? Maybe at the reception?"

She made a face. "Ah, no."

"Have you ever had champagne?"

"Only once, and it wasn't pretty."

Nick laughed. "What about the toast to the bride?"

"I don't think she'll mind if I stick to mineral water."

"I'm sure she won't mind a bit."

These days when he spoke about his sister, it was with genuine affection. In so many ways he was a different person from the man she'd met three weeks ago. Earlier in the week she'd reminded him to call Leslie about the tuxedo fitting, and he'd ended up taking his sister out for lunch. Just the two of them, and it had even been his idea. And last night he'd gone willingly, if not altogether happily, to the rehearsal dinner. He'd asked Maggie to go with him but she had declined, since she hadn't been formally invited. The last thing she wanted to do was to give Mrs. Durrance a reason to dislike her.

"But if you need to propose another toast to your aunt, a gin gimlet might be necessary, no?" He was back to teasing again.

She fingered the strand of pearls. "No. I think she would be the last person to expect me to do something like that."

"A wise woman, your aunt Margaret." He pulled up behind two long white limos parked in front of the church. "Take the umbrella and go inside while I find a place to park. If you see Leslie, tell her I'll be right in. She's probably wearing out the carpet, worried that I'll screw up."

Maggie touched his arm. "I think It's very sweet that she wants you to do this. I'm sure it means a lot to her."

"I'm still surprised she asked," he said. "But I'm glad she did."

Maggie leaned forward and gave him a light kiss on the cheek. "I know you are."

"And how do you know that?"

"I just do." She looked at the ivy-covered facade of the old church. "What a perfect place for a wedding." She opened the car door, stuck the umbrella outside and released the catch, then stepped beneath it. "See you inside."

Hoping the rain wouldn't ruin her shoes, she dashed up the church steps and through the carved wooden doors, collapsing her umbrella as she went. She adored weddings and she'd been looking forward to this one ever since Nick had invited her. Organ music drifted into the empty foyer. Two ushers stood just beyond the double doors that led to the main part of the church, which was filled with wedding guests. The dripping umbrella had created a surprisingly large puddle on the floor and she was looking for a place to stash it when the bride rushed down a corridor toward her.

"Leslie! What an amazing dress! You look gorgeous." She also looked frantic. "It's my fault we're late. I'm so sorry. Nick will be right in. He's just parking the car."

Leslie grabbed her hand and squeezed it between both of hers. Her fingers were ice-cold and trembling. "Maggie, I'm so glad I found you. Allison told me how much you helped her and I could really use some advice right now."

"Of course. What's up?"

"What should a person do when the right thing doesn't feel right?" she asked.

Maggie didn't hesitate. "Let your heart guide you. Your head will always look for reasons to explain away the doubt but it can never change what you know in your heart."

Leslie hugged her, wet umbrella and all. "Thank you! You're a lifesaver." Then she dashed back down the hallway.

Maggie looked through the open double doors. The gray-haired minister stood in front of the altar, and Gerald and John were taking their places. They both looked quite dashing, but neither of them could hold a candle to Nick.

"Maggie?" Nick stood just inside the doorway, holding a soggy newspaper over his head. "Man, it's raining harder than ever."

She brushed the raindrops from his broad shoulders. "Did I tell you how good you look?"

He smiled down at her. "You might have mentioned it. Do you know where Leslie is?"

"Down there." She pointed down the corridor Leslie had taken. "She was just here looking for you and I told her it was all my fault that you're late. Wait until you see her. She looks amazing."

"You should go in," he said, pointing to one of the ushers. "Tell Martin you're with me. And my mother."

She blew Nick a kiss, hoping it covered her sudden bout of nerves, and accepted the arm of a man she remembered meeting at Allison's barbecue.

The church was packed, and filled with the sound of organ music and hushed voices. Maggie had never seen so many flowers in one room. The end of each pew was decked out with white lilies, gardenias and trailing peach-colored ribbons and the altar was all but obscured by giant white flower-filled urns. The florist must have planned his retirement when this order came in.

Maggie wasn't sure if it was the flowers or the music or the way people's heads turned to look at her as she passed, but suddenly she was imagining a very different wedding. The man at her side was the shadowy image of her father, dignified in his navy pinstriped suit. The thin, pale man standing near the altar was replaced by Nick, looking devastatingly handsome in his tuxedo.

She'd never considered having a traditional wedding, but it could be fun. Her mother would come from Manhattan. Nick's family would be here. Her father would be here in spirit and, of course, Aunt Margaret wouldn't miss it. It would be perfect.

The usher stopped at the second pew from the front and indicated that's where she should sit. Her fantasy wedding was abruptly halted by a pair of cold gray eyes.

"Here?" she whispered to the man at her side.

He nodded.

Yikes. This was Nick's mother?

Maggie sat and held out her hand. "Hello," she whispered "I'm Maggie Meadowcroft."

The woman's rigid posture stiffened some more. "I know who you are." Her hands remained firmly clasped in her lap.

So that's how it was going to be. Maggie propped the umbrella against the edge of the pew, chiding herself for not leaving the miserable thing in the foyer as it made yet another puddle. Not much she could do about it now, but she could tuck it under the seat with her handbag where it would be out of the way.

Her purse bumped the umbrella, which toppled sideways and crashed to the floor, narrowly missing the toe of one of Mrs. Durrance's ivory-satin pumps.

"Sorry," she whispered, avoiding eye contact with Nick's mother as she shoved the purse and umbrella under the pew.

She twisted her strand of pearls around one finger, hoping the ceremony would start soon and trying to figure out how to thaw Mrs. Durrance's frosty disposition once the reception was under way.

Ten minutes later, the organist was playing Pachelbel's "Canon," again, and the hushed conversations of the people in the church grew louder. Every few minutes Maggie glanced over her shoulder and saw that everyone else was doing the same. Mrs. Durrance kept her unwavering gaze on something at the front of the church. If she was concerned by the delay, she covered it well. Even the low, distant rumble of thunder didn't seem to faze her.

Maggie studied the huge stained-glass window that rose up to the arched ceiling. She was contemplating Gabriel's magnificence and the surprising length of time that had passed since she'd taken her seat when she felt a light tap on her shoulder.

Nick leaned close. "Come with me," he whispered. "We need you at the back for a minute."

"What's wrong?" his mother asked.

"Nothing. We just need Maggie's help with something." But judging by his hard-set jaw and narrowed eyes, something was very wrong.

What could it be?

The groom stepped forward and grabbed Nick's arm. "What

the hell's going on?" The words hissed sharply from between his teeth. "It's time to get this show on the road. People are starting to talk."

Nick gripped his shoulder. "Why don't you—"

"Gentlemen." Mrs. Durrance cleared her throat. "You—" she pointed at Gerald, then made a subtle gesture toward the altar "—get back up there and set an example."

An example of what? Maggie wondered. Surely she wasn't the only one thinking that maybe there wasn't going to be a wedding.

Oh, dear Lord! That's not what she'd been thinking. The idea had just popped into her head that very moment. Is that what Gerald meant when he said people were starting to talk?

If it was possible there wasn't going to be a wedding this morning, Mrs. Durrance hadn't caught on. Yet. "I don't know what's going on and I don't want to know," she said. "I'm here for my daughter's wedding. Make it happen."

Nick didn't reply. Instead he took Maggie's arm and she tried to keep up with his long strides as he hurried her up the aisle. She pasted on a bright smile and tried to ignore all the curious glances.

"Is something wrong?" she asked as soon as they stepped into the foyer.

"Leslie's gone."

She'd had no idea what the problem might be, but she hadn't expected him to say that. "She's here. I saw her."

"That's why I came to get you. I think you were the last person to see her."

Uh-oh. Maggie didn't like the sound of that.

"This is not like Leslie. How was she when you spoke to her? Did you get the impression she was ready to take off?"

Leslie had asked what a person should do when doing the right thing didn't feel right. At the time it had sounded like a perfectly normal question from a jittery bride.

"Are you sure she's gone?"

"If she's here, I can't find her. Did she say anything to you?"

How do I always end up in the middle of these things? Maggie asked herself. "She seemed nervous, but that's normal, don't you think? I mean, I've never been a bride so I really can't say for sure if it's normal but—"

"Maggie!" His hands curved gently over her shoulders. "We don't have time for this. I have to find Leslie and it looks as though you're the last person who spoke to her. I need to know what she said."

"She asked what I thought a person should do when doing the right thing doesn't feel right."

"And?"

"That's it."

"What do you think she meant?"

Maggie shrugged, liking the weight of his hands on her shoulders. "I'm not sure."

"What did you tell her?"

"To listen to her heart instead of her head."

"Hmm."

That was all he said, and she had no idea what he was thinking. "I assumed she was having last-minute jitters, not second thoughts."

"Would that have changed the advice you gave her?"

"No." She gave the answer without hesitation.

Nick heaved a sigh. "I didn't think so."

"You think this is my fault?"

He gave her a long, thoughtful look and Maggie felt her chest tighten.

"Of course not," he said finally. "But if she said anything more specific, you'd tell me, wouldn't you?"

"You think I'd hide something like that from you?"

He looked uncomfortable. "You might, if she asked you to."

"Why would she confide in me? She hardly knows me."

He shrugged. "For the same reason everyone else is doing it."

"Actually," she said cautiously, "I don't know that many people in Collingwood Station."

"Plenty of people already know who *you* are, and they're saying…" He hesitated. "Never mind. I need to find Leslie. Maybe we should talk to Allison and Candice again."

They hurried down the corridor and into a small room where the bridesmaids were waiting.

Allison was rearranging the baby's breath in her daughter's hair while her son sat on a chair reading a comic book. She glanced up when they walked in. "Any sign of her?"

Nick shook his head.

"What if something has happened?"

For heaven's sake, Maggie thought. What was it with these people and drama? "I'm sure she's fine, but she did seem upset when I saw her."

Allison shot an accusatory look at Nick. "She said she was going to look for her brother. The ceremony was supposed to start in a few minutes and she was getting worried he wouldn't show up. Maybe if you'd been on time, this wouldn't have "

"Don't even think about trying to pin this on me. Leslie wouldn't run out on her own wedding because I was a few minutes late."

Maggie had one of those niggly feelings deep inside that told her something else was going on here. She wasn't sure what it was, but it had nothing to do with Nick. "The first thing I told her was that Nick was parking the car. Well, no, the first thing I said was that she looked beautiful, then I told her about Nick. She seemed to calm down after we talked and she came back down this hallway."

Allison gave a dramatic shrug. "She didn't come here."

Nick turned to Candice, who was fidgeting with the ribbons on her bouquet.

That woman really needs to learn to relax, Maggie thought.

"Don't look at me," Candice said. "I was in the little girl's room." Yet for some reason that didn't ring true, and she even sounded a little defensive.

"Maybe Leslie went to the little girl's room, too?" Maggie suggested while she watched for Candice's reaction.

The woman shook her head, but wouldn't make eye contact.

Maggie's patience was running out, which rarely happened. "She was upset about something more important than us being a few minutes late. And it's pouring outside. Did she have a car here?"

"No," Allison said. "We all rode together in one of the limos."

"They're both still parked out front," Nick said. "I checked."

"She couldn't have left through the front door," Maggie said. "One of us would have seen her."

"There's a side exit near the minister's office. I'll go check that."

Candice got up from her chair in a swish of peach-colored silk. "I'll help look for her."

Maggie and Allison exchanged doubtful glances. "I'm sure everything will be fine," Maggie said, trying to sound bright and cheerful. Meanwhile the bad feeling that had been gnawing at her insides had worked its way up her chest and clogged her throat.

If Leslie was having second thoughts, had Maggie's last-minute counsel tipped the balance? She didn't feel guilty about preventing a bad marriage, yet she had a horrible feeling that she'd done something wrong.

There's no sense borrowing trouble.

Recalling Aunt Margaret's sage advice usually made her feel better, but not this time.

Nick returned with a rain-drenched bouquet in his hand. "Found this outside."

Maggie's heart sank. "What are you going to do?"

He tossed the soggy mess onto a table. "Guess I'll start by telling everyone there isn't going to be a wedding."

"Do you want me to go with you?" Maggie asked. *Please say no,* she thought. She didn't want to be in the same room as Mrs. Durrance when Nick delivered that news.

"No. Stay here with Allison." He released a heavy sigh and headed back out the door.

"Leslie will *never* live this down," Allison said. "Maybe your secret little makeover project should have included the whole Durrance family instead of just Nick."

"Ssshhh!" Maggie glanced across the room and cringed.

Nick was back, looming in the doorway. His face, which a moment ago had shown so much concern for his sister, was overwritten by stunned belief.

On second thought, make that anger.

"What did you say?" he asked Allison.

She laughed nervously, as if trying to brush aside her thoughtless comment. "Don't take everything so seriously, Nick. It was a joke."

He clearly wasn't buying it. He turned on Maggie. "A 'project'? What the hell is that supposed to mean?"

Her sixth sense had let her down this time. She had never imagined that Allison would let that slip out and she was completely unprepared for Nick's anger. "I know it sounds bad—"

"Sounds bad? It *is* bad. People aren't like houses. You don't get to renovate them into…" He hesitated, as though he was trying to figure what she wanted him to be.

"If you'll let me explain, you'll see that I wasn't trying to make you into anything. I love you just the way you are. I only want you to be happy."

He stared at her, and during those few seconds, Maggie clung to her last remaining hope.

"Do I look happy?" he asked finally.

She shook her head, unable to speak. *Don't let them see you cry,* she said to herself. *Don't let them see you cry.*

"As if this day wasn't already bad enough, I find out that you told her—" he paused and waved an arm at Allison "—her, of all people, that I'm some kind of project. Welcome to Collingwood Station." He practically shouted it. "You're going to fit right in with the rest of the busybodies in this town."

Allison hustled her children out of the room. Maggie clutched the lapels of Nick's jacket, desperate to make him understand. "I wasn't meddling, I was trying to help."

That only seemed to make him even angrier. "Did I ask for your help?"

She shook her head, not exactly sure what she needed to say to fix this. "You don't understand. I don't see how you can blame me for something Allison said—"

"You don't see how I can blame you? Why doesn't that surprise me? Maybe you should talk this over with your dead aunt or read your horoscope or…or go gaze into your crystal ball. Maybe that'll help you figure out why you should mind your own damn business and stay out of mine."

"I don't have a crystal ball."

"Ahhhh! You just don't get it, do you?" His hands wrapped around her wrists. His touch was gentle, and for a moment she thought he'd started to calm down. Then he pushed her away as he stepped back. "I have to go call off a wedding."

He left the room before she had a chance to respond.

Chapter Fourteen

Maggie fumbled her way into a chair. Half an hour ago, everything had been perfect. She had finally fallen in love with a man who'd wanted to be with her, too, but in typical Maggie Meadowcroft style, she'd blown it.

She wished she could feel sorry for herself, but all of this was her fault. She should never, ever have said anything to Allison about Nick.

What had she been thinking?

Look before you leap. Aunt Margaret had issued that warning every time she'd done something crazy, but she never seemed to learn. She covered her face with her hands and felt the pearls brush against her wrists. Suddenly she was desperate to get home. Aunt Margaret would know what she should do.

She jumped up and rushed into the corridor, but people were already streaming out of the church and into the foyer. No way could she face anyone, especially not Nick and his mother. He'd said there was a side door near the minister's office. She'd slip out that way and be on her way before anyone decided to come look for her. Not that anyone was likely to.

The door led to the parking lot. It was still pouring rain, which reminded her that she'd left her purse and umbrella under her seat in the church. Too bad, she thought. She definitely wasn't going back to collect them.

She dashed across the parking lot, relieved to see that none of the wedding guests had made their way outside yet. She ran around to the back of the church, hoping no one noticed her, and crossed the street. Since she was already soaking wet, she might as well walk home.

That's when she spotted the little red sports car parked along-side the curb. Was that Candice behind the wheel?

Maggie slowed as she passed it. Yes, it was Candice, all right, leaning toward the man in the passenger seat. And not just any man. It was the groom.

What was he doing out here?

Kind of a stupid question, Maggie thought, since Candice had her tongue in his mouth and he had his hand down the front of her dress.

How on earth had they managed to get out of the church so quickly? And what were they doing together?

At that instant, everything crystalized in Maggie's mind. The love spell she'd cast for Candice had worked, with devastating consequences.

Had Leslie figured out what was going on? Considering their lack of discretion—even Mr. Donaldson had seen them together!—that was entirely possible. If so, no wonder she bolted.

Maggie arrived home, soaked to the skin. And as if the day wasn't already the biggest disaster, her keys were in the stupid purse she'd left at the stupid church. She dashed around the house and retrieved the spare from under a plant pot on the back porch.

Nick probably wouldn't approve of the stashed key, since he thought she should keep her front door locked and not let anyone in until she knew who was there.

Correction.

An hour ago, he wouldn't have approved. Now he couldn't care less.

She let herself in the front door and went upstairs. She wanted to sit and have a good cry, but she needed to figure out what had gone wrong with the love spell.

Why did every disaster seem to be so much worse than the last one? She could learn from her mistakes—in fact, she never made the same one twice. But who could have predicted that Candice would hook up with Leslie's fiancé? Maggie wouldn't have believed it if she hadn't seen it with her own eyes.

She peeled off the wet dress and hung it over the bathtub to drip.

What was it that Mr. Donaldson had said? *Not a lot goes on in this town that I don't know about. I don't go in for gossip, but I've got eyes.*

In her bedroom, she put on dry underwear and pulled on a pair of jeans and her purple tie-dyed T-shirt.

She went across the hall and pulled the yearbook off the shelf. What a disaster of a day this had been.

Well, I've never been one to say I told you so, but this kind of meddling always leads to no good.

Aunt Margaret had always been very quick with the I-told-you-so's.

"You know what? I'm having a really, *really* bad day and I'd rather not talk about it."

Humph. A bad day is having a your car break down in rush-hour traffic. Ruining a wedding and having your boyfriend dump you sounds more like a train wreck if you ask me.

"I didn't ruin the wedding and Nick is not my boyfriend." And now there was no chance he ever would be.

He'll be back, mark my words.

"I don't think so, Aunt Margaret. Not this time."

Don't be too quick to give up on him. Besides, I'm getting tired of hanging around. I've been hoping he'd stick around and look after you.

"I don't need to be looked after."

Because you do such a good job of keeping yourself out of trouble?

"Please, Aunt Margaret. Not now."

She didn't want to dwell on all the trouble she'd caused, or listen to one of her aunt's lectures. But she did want to go back over the stupid spell she'd done for Candice and try to figure out what went wrong. Then she'd have to call her mother—and listen to a few more I-told-you-so's—and find a way to undo this mess. Not that Leslie was likely to want her fiancé back, or that Nick would ever speak to her again, but at least she'd know for next time.

Next time? You can't be serious.

Aunt Margaret was right. "Fine. I've learned my lesson and there won't be a next time." Unfortunately there would never be another Nick, either.

NICK SLAMMED THE DOOR of his apartment, threw his keys onto the counter, tossed Maggie's purse next to it and tried to think of when he'd ever had a worse day.

Nope. This topped the list.

He yanked open the fridge and grabbed a beer. The cap jangled across the counter after his keys. He took a long swig and set the bottle on the counter. Smashing it against the Formica would have been a lot more satisfying, but he didn't dare let himself lose control. If he lost it, he might…

What? Track down Gerald and use as much force as necessary to make the guy tell him what he'd done to Leslie. Although now that he'd had a chance to cool off a little, he had to admit that this was as much his fault as anyone's. He'd had a bad feeling when he'd seen Gerald and Candice together at the barbecue. He should have said something to Leslie. Instead, he'd turned a blind eye and it had been Maggie who'd set her straight.

Maggie.

Thinking about her made him angry all over again. Turning him into one of her projects was one the most harebrained, infuriating things anyone had ever done to him. What the hell had she been thinking? He'd thought he was falling in love with her, in spite of all her crazy ideas about ghosts and horoscopes and yogurt facials. Maybe even because of them. Why did she have to meddle in his life? She knew how much he hated busybodies and yet she'd...

Aw, hell.

He couldn't think of what she'd done, specifically, but now that he thought about it, she'd done something. She must have, because he felt different. Happier. More settled. Just a week ago he'd had an almost-civil conversation with his mother. And since the Fourth of July barbecue, he and Leslie had been closer than they'd ever been. Before Maggie, there was no way those things would have happened. He couldn't put his finger on it, exactly, but she had something to do with all the changes in his life. That's not what he was mad about, though. What bugged him was the way she...

What?

He grabbed the beer and took another long drink while he tried to think of something that bugged him.

Making him into a project. She'd even admitted it. In truth, he didn't completely understand what that meant. She'd never said or done anything that felt like she was interfering, but that didn't make it all right.

Whatever "it" was.

Damn.

He picked up the beer bottle and poured its contents down the sink. This was not a good time to tie one on. Especially not alone.

He should call Brent, that's what he should do. Then as soon as he got himself out of this monkey suit, they could go out for a few beers, maybe shoot some pool. Brent would make sure he didn't do anything stupid.

He yanked off his tie as he made his way to the phone. The flashing light indicated there were messages. Maybe Maggie had come to her senses and called to apologize.

He dialed into voice mail and switched to speaker phone while he opened the top button of his shirt.

"Nick? It's Leslie. I wanted to let you know I'm all right and to say I'm sorry for what happened this morning."

That was followed by a long pause and he thought he could hear her sniffling in the background. And was that a dog barking? Then she was talking again.

"I couldn't go through with it, not after I saw…well, I just couldn't. I need to ask a favor though. Well, one more, since I imagine you've already had to deal with all those people. And Mother. Anyway, could you please tell—"

Beep.

Damn.

Next message.

"Nick, sorry, it's me again. I was cut off. I wanted to ask you to talk to Maggie for me and thank her for everything. I'm not sure what happened but since she's been around, you and I… things have been better, you know what I mean? More like family should be. And this morning at the church, she told me to follow my heart. No one's ever told me that before, but she was right. She's an amazing woman, Nick. You're very lucky, but I guess you already know that. Anyway, I'm going to stay out of sight for a while but I don't want you to worry. And can you let Mother know that I'm okay? I can't talk to her right now. Not that it'll make a difference, anyway. I'll call in a few days. Please give Maggie a hug for me."

Beep.

Next message.

Now what?

"Nick. Brent here. Something's come up. Sorry to leave you in the lurch, buddy, but I'll give you a call in a couple of days. See ya."

Beep.

Nick disconnected and stared at the phone. How was that for a weird coincidence? Leslie and Brent doing a disappearing act at the same time.

"What difference does it make?" he said out loud. It's not as though he needed any more to think about.

He supposed he should let his mother know he'd heard from Leslie, but it'd take more than a few beers to put him in the mood for that conversation. Leslie's welfare would have a low priority until Lydia Durrance had made up a story that would help her save face.

What to do about Maggie was another matter.

He couldn't pin the wedding fiasco on her. On the other hand, she'd turned him into one of her makeover projects, for God's sake. And as if that wasn't bad enough, she'd told Allison. Which meant the whole damn town knew about it. After all these years, he still hated being gossiped about.

If she had just left well enough alone, they'd be together right now. She in that fabulous dress and the pearls, or out of them. No denying it, no matter how aggravating she was, he still wanted to be with her.

I love you just the way you are.

He swore under his breath. He loved her, too. He'd never met anyone like her and he wanted to spend the rest of his life with her. If he had any kind of backbone, he'd tell her. Too bad he'd been in such a big hurry last week to finish the reno on her house because it meant he no longer had an excuse to see her.

Except that he had her purse. His curiosity nearly got the best of him, but he decided against looking inside. As long as he didn't know its contents, he could assume there might be something in it that she needed right away.

Which meant he'd better get it over there, asap.

NICK STEPPED OUT of his truck and looked up at Maggie's house. The mauve siding and purple trim wouldn't have been his first choice and he never would have thought to paint the front door red, but it all worked and it suited her to a tee. Maggie knew what she wanted and she wasn't afraid to go for it.

The gate swung shut behind him with perfect precision. The new steps had been painted dark purple to match the trim and at both ends of each tread Maggie had set big terra-cotta pots filled with red and yellow and purple flowers.

He lifted the heavy brass door knocker and held it for a moment before he let it drop. Had it really only been a month since he'd come here, thinking his old high-school teacher wanted to hire him? He could hardly remember life before Maggie.

He let the grinning gargoyle fall against the brass plate and waited.

Maybe she wasn't home. Or maybe she didn't want to see him.

He still had a key, but this would not be a good time to use it. If she'd even bothered to lock the door. He resisted the temptation to try the knob and knocked again.

"Come in!"

Maggie, Maggie, Maggie. She was way too trusting, and that was never going to change.

He let himself in. No scent of fruity concoctions this time, only fresh paint and oiled woodwork.

He knew she'd be in the kitchen. He found her leaning over the table, pouring over several of her notebooks. Her damp hair hung around her shoulders and a pang of guilt shot through him when he realized she must have walked home in the rain. She was barefoot and wearing an old pair of jeans and the purple shirt she'd had on that first day. And her aunt's necklace.

"I thought you might need your purse," he said.

She swung around, obviously surprised to see him.

"And I was wrong about the pearls," he said. "They look great with tie-dye."

She didn't say anything, so he continued. "I also came here to apologize. I'm still not sure I understand what Allison meant, but—"

Maggie's vigorous head shaking interrupted him. "Never mind that. I have to confess, I've done something terrible. Really, really terrible. Leslie calling off the wedding…it's all my fault."

Now what? he wondered. He moved slowly across the kitchen toward her. "She called a while ago and left a message. She didn't say where she was, but she sounded okay."

Maggie brightened a little. "I'm glad."

"She asked me to thank you. She said your advice was exactly what she needed to hear." He paused and mustered his courage. "She also said I was lucky to have you in my life. I've known that for a while now, but today I let myself forget."

Maggie wouldn't let him continue. "I don't deserve an apology. I was trying to help Allison…and I did…but I ended up ruining Leslie's wedding in the process."

He wasn't sure he wanted to know how helping Allison could ruin his sister's wedding, but he knew he was about to find out anyway. "Leslie's message was pretty clear. She said you gave her the right advice and that she wanted me to pass along her thanks."

"She only said that because she doesn't know what I've done."

Nick sighed. He wanted to put his arms around her and kiss her until she forgot about everyone else's problems, but in the past few weeks he'd learned that when she got like this, the best thing to do was to hear her out. Then kiss her. "Why don't you tell me what you think you've done, and we'll figure out a way to fix it?"

"Remember the barbecue at Allison's?"

"Sure."

"And it seemed as though Candice had a thing for Allison's husband?"

"Yes," he repeated cautiously while his gut tied itself in a knot. Candice had also seemed to have a "thing" for Gerald that night, and he'd dismissed it as being none of his business.

"The next day you started to work here and all the noise was totally distracting, so I went over to Allison's."

"Right. I remember." At the time he'd been relieved because it had meant Allison wouldn't show up at Maggie's.

"I could tell she'd been crying but she wouldn't admit it. You know how she is, always so—"

"Maggie?" If she got sidetracked, who knew when she'd get to the point.

"Yes?"

"Can you stick to the story?"

"Of course. Sorry. When I asked if I could help, she said something very strange. She asked if I knew any love spells."

Dear God, please let there be a point to this. "I'm surprised Allison believes in stuff like that."

"She doesn't. At least, I don't think she was serious, but I got to thinking—"

"That you'd do a love spell anyway?" Even as he said it, he could hardly believe he was having this conversation. "She already has a husband so wouldn't that be, oh, I don't know. Redundant?"

"Not if it made her husband fall in love with her all over again," Maggie said, looking surprised that he had to ask. "You know, so he wouldn't be interested in Candice."

Of course. That made perfect sense. Not. "What does this have to do with Leslie?"

"We-eell, I called my mother and I explained the situation to her. She knows a lot about these things, so—"

Now, that would have been an interesting conversation. Nick forced back a laugh by clearing his throat. "Your mother makes love potions?"

"Love spells, actually. And she's very good at it. We decided that John was probably still in love with Allison, so fixing their relationship would be easy. And it was. All I had to do was to sneak it into their house and hide it under their bed."

She could not be serious. "You broke into their house?"

"No! John let me in because I told him I wanted to see how Allison had decorated their upstairs bathroom and—"

Nick put up a hand. Not that anything about Maggie really surprised him anymore, but that kind of highjinks was way more information than he needed to know.

"Neither of them suspected a thing. And the spell worked."

He detected an unspoken "so there" at the end of that declaration. "How do you know it worked?"

"Because the next morning they started building the tree house together and they were obviously really happy."

At least now he knew why Maggie had given him the brush-off the night before. "You might not want to hear this, but John talked to me earlier that week about building the tree house. It was already in the works."

"But they were certainly happy that day."

Nick sighed. Yes, they were, and if Maggie wanted to take the credit for that, what was the harm in letting her?

She shrugged off her disappointment. "Gabriella, my mother, thought it would be best to create a really potent spell for Candice so she would find a man of her own, fall in love and leave Allison's husband alone. She knew a spell that didn't require the actual presence of the person, just a photograph."

She pointed to the Collingwood Station yearbook on the table.

He would have laughed out loud, except that Maggie was completely serious. "You used Candice's high-school picture?"

She nodded.

"Okay. But I still don't see how that affects Leslie."

"Look at the page."

Nick stepped up to the table and stood close enough so that Maggie's shoulder touched his arm. He looked at Candice's photograph. It was partly obscured by a reddish-brown stain.

"I had to set up some candles around the picture on the first Friday after the full moon and recite an incantation. My mother warned me about this spell and I should have listened, but I had no idea it was so powerful."

"Maggie, I'm sure this stuff seems real to you, but—"

"You won't be such a skeptic when I tell you what happened."

Nick sighed. She'd get to the end of this story sooner if he humored her. "Then I guess you'd better tell."

She took a long breath.

"The short version," he said, even though he knew she'd tell it her way and there wasn't a damn thing he could do about it.

"I didn't want to cut up Aunt Margaret's yearbook so I laid it open on the table and set up the candles around it. After I lit one of them, I accidentally knocked it over, but I didn't think that would be problem, so I just set up everything again and recited the incantation. But now I see that some of the wax dripped on the photograph next to Candice's."

She pointed to the page.

Sure enough there was another waxy stain, right smack in the middle of Gerald Bedford's face. "And you think that's what got Gerald and Candice together?"

"What other explanation could there be?"

He could think of several. As for Maggie, she was so convinced she had all this power, and he loved her for it, but was there any way to ease her conscience without bursting her bubble? "Okay," he said cautiously. "Let me get this straight. By putting that stuff on the two pictures, whether you meant to or not, you brought those two together?"

She looked relieved. "Yes! I'm such a klutz. I had no idea what I'd done until it was too late. I saw them when I left the church a while ago. They were together in Candice's car and they were making out."

He closed the book. "I have a confession to make, too, and I think it's going to make your confession obsolete."

"Obsolete?"

He nodded. "I'm afraid so. The night of Allison's barbecue, I saw Gerald and Candice together."

Maggie's eyes went wide.

"Gerald went into the house and Candice followed him a few minutes later. I didn't think much of it until I saw them come back outside a while later, just after the fireworks, when we were leaving."

"You mean they'd been—"

"That's what I mean."

"But you don't know for sure."

"No. I don't seem to be equipped with any of your sixth sense, but I do have a brain. If I'd been using it, I would have said something to my sister."

"Why didn't you?"

"I told myself it was none of my business. I mean, I didn't think she should marry that guy under any circumstances but who was I to tell her that?"

"Well, you are her brother."

He shrugged. "And a pretty lousy one, but what else is new?"

"That's not true."

While Maggie absorbed what he'd just told her, he took advantage of her preoccupation to put his arms around her. He was tired of talking about other people.

She looked up at him. "So you think they were...you know...before I did the love spell?"

"I'd say they were definitely...you know."

"So I didn't—"

"Ruin Leslie's wedding?" He decided to let her down easy. "I'm afraid you can't take any credit for that."

"I still feel badly about what happened. Besides, what if what you saw was just a coincidence? They might have noticed each other but they probably wouldn't have fallen in love if—"

"Who said anything about love? Those two aren't capable of having feelings for anyone but themselves. Besides, if Gerald had suddenly fallen in love with Candice—" Oh, man, he couldn't believe they were having this conversation "—why do you think was he still going to marry my sister?"

Her eyes went narrow. "I'm not sure."

"I'll tell you why. Because he's a self-centered jerk. He thought he could have it all. A beautiful, successful wife. A trampy mistress."

The disillusioned look in Maggie's eyes made him stop.

"And why was Leslie the one to call off the wedding?" he asked.

"Maybe she saw them together. Candice and John weren't being very discreet. Or maybe she just sensed something wasn't right."

"Trust me, my sister is no more equipped with a sixth sense than I am." He smoothed the damp hair away from Maggie's face. "You, on the other hand, have an amazing way with people, Maggie Meadowcroft. I think you got Leslie to think about whether being married to Gerald was what she really wanted, and the answer was no."

"What about you? Have you thought about what you want?"

"Oh, yeah."

"And?"

He took in the beautiful woman standing in front of him. "I like what I see, and…I like my life the way it is. So whatever you had in mind for a makeover, you can just forget it. You'll have to take me the way I am."

"The way you are, huh?" There was that smug little smile again.

"What are you grinning about?" he asked.

"Nothing. If you're happy, then so am I."

"So are we through talking about everyone else's love life?"

She nodded and her gorgeous brown eyes were filled with promise. Finally.

"Good."

He tilted her chin up and kissed her.

"Nick?" she said against his lips.

"What?"

"I'm sorry for saying anything to Allison. And I've definitely sworn off meddling."

"Shh. We're finished talking, remember?" He was ready for some action, and Maggie's response suggested he was on the right track.

"Fine," she whispered. "No more talking."

She kissed him back, and he knew right then that this was for real. That no matter what kind of crazy ideas she had about love spells and ghosts…

He backed off a little and looked at her. "Your aunt isn't hanging around here, is she?"

Maggie tilted her head a little and glanced around the room, but she couldn't hide the mischief in her eyes. "No sign of her. She told me she was getting tired and that I needed to find someone else to look after me."

He ran a finger over the strand of pearls. "And you haven't cast a spell on me?"

She shook her head.

"Do you swear you'll never try one?"

"I swear."

"Good. Because I'd like to think I've fallen in love with you without any interference from anybody. Not even you."

Her eyes went wide. "You're in love with me?"

"Isn't it obvious?"

She seemed to give that some thought. "It is now." Then she pointed to the yearbook. "It says in there that your favorite pastime is breaking hearts."

"I didn't write that."

"So it isn't true?"

"You know, no one ever asked if I had my heart broken. How do I know you won't break it?"

"I don't break hearts. I only mend them."

"Then I'd say we're both in good hands."

* * * * *

Want to know what happened to Leslie?
Find out in Lee McKenzie's next book,
WITH THIS RING,
coming December 2007,
only from Harlequin American Romance!

THE ROYAL HOUSE OF NIROLI
Always passionate, always proud

The richest royal family in the world—united by blood and passion, torn apart by deceit and desire.

Nestled in the azure blue of the Mediterranean Sea, the majestic island of Niroli has prospered for centuries. The Fierezza men have worn the crown with passion and pride since ancient times. But now, as the king's health declines and his two sons have been tragically killed, the crown is in jeopardy.

The clock is ticking—a new heir must be found before the king is forced to abdicate. By royal decree the internationally scattered members of the Fierezza family are summoned to claim their destiny. But any person who takes the throne must do so according to The Rules of the Royal House of Niroli. Soon secrets and rivalries emerge as the descendents of this ancient royal line vie for position and power. Only a true Fierezza can become ruler—a person dedicated to their country, their people…and their eternal love!

Each month starting in July 2007,
Harlequin Presents is delighted to bring you
an exciting installment from
THE ROYAL HOUSE OF NIROLI,
in which you can follow the epic search
for the true Nirolian king.
Eight heirs, eight romances, eight fantastic stories!

Here's your chance to enjoy a sneak preview of the first book delivered to you by royal decree….

FIVE minutes later she was standing immobile in front of the study's window, her original purpose of coming in forgotten, as she stared in shocked horror at the envelope she was holding. Waves of heat followed by icy chills surged through her body. She could hardly see the address now through her blurred vision, but the crest on its left-hand front corner stood out, its *royal* crest, followed by the address: *HRH Prince Marco of Niroli...*

She didn't hear Marco's key in the apartment door, she didn't even hear him calling out her name. Her shock was so great that nothing could penetrate it. It encased her in a kind of bubble, which only concentrated the torment of what she was suffering and branded it on her brain so that it could never be forgotten. It was only finally pierced by the sudden opening of the study door as Marco walked in.

"Welcome home, *Your Highness.* I suppose I ought to curtsy." She waited, praying that he would laugh and tell her that she had got it all wrong, that the envelope she was holding, addressing him as Prince Marco of Niroli, was some silly mistake. But like a tiny candle flame shivering vulnerably in the dark, her hope trembled fearfully. And then the look in Marco's eyes extinguished it as cruelly as a hand placed callously over a dying person's face to stem their last breath.

"Give that to me," he demanded, taking the envelope from her.

"It's too late, Marco," Emily told him brokenly. "I know the truth now…." She dug her teeth in her lower lip to try to force back her own pain.

"You had no right to go through my desk," Marco shot back at her furiously, full of loathing at being caught off guard and forced into a position in which he was in the wrong, making him determined to find something he could accuse Emily of. "I trusted you…."

Emily could hardly believe what she was hearing. "No, you didn't trust me, Marco, and you didn't trust me because you knew that I couldn't trust you. And you knew that because you're a liar, and liars don't trust people because they know that they themselves cannot be trusted." She not only felt sick, she also felt as though she could hardly breathe. "You are Prince Marco of Niroli… How could you not tell me who you are and still live with me as intimately as we have lived together?" she demanded brokenly.

"Stop being so ridiculously dramatic," Marco demanded fiercely. "You are making too much of the situation."

"*Too much?*" Emily almost screamed the words at him. "When were you going to tell me, Marco? Perhaps you just planned to walk away without telling me anything? After all, what do my feelings matter to you?"

"Of course they matter." Marco stopped her sharply. "And it was in part to protect them—and you—that I decided not to inform you when my grandfather first announced that he intended to step down from the throne and hand it on to me."

"To protect me?" Emily nearly choked on her fury. "Hand on the throne? No wonder you told me when you first took me to bed that all you wanted was sex. You *knew* that was the only kind of relationship there could ever be between us! You *knew* that one day you would be Niroli's king. No doubt you are expected to marry a princess. Is she picked out for you already, your *royal* bride?"

* * * * *

Look for THE FUTURE KING'S PREGNANT MISTRESS
by Penny Jordan in July 2007,
from Harlequin Presents,
available wherever books are sold.

HARLEQUIN®

Mediterranean NIGHTS™

Experience the glamour and elegance of cruising the high seas with a new 12-book series....

MEDITERRANEAN NIGHTS

Coming in July 2007...

SCENT OF A WOMAN

by

Joanne Rock

When Danielle Chevalier is invited to an exclusive conference aboard *Alexandra's Dream,* she knows it will mean good things for her struggling fragrance company. But her dreams get a setback when she meets Adam Burns, a representative from a large American conglomerate.

Danielle is charmed by the brusque American—until she finds out he means to compete with her bid for the opportunity that will save her family business!

nocturne™

**DON'T MISS THE RIVETING CONCLUSION
TO THE RAINTREE TRILOGY**

RAINTREE: SANCTUARY

by *New York Times* bestselling author

BEVERLY BARTON

Mercy, guardian of the Raintree
homeplace, takes a stand against
the Ansara wizards to battle for
the Clan's future.

*On sale July,
wherever books are sold.*

SNRT2

THE GARRISONS

A brand-new family saga begins with

THE CEO'S SCANDALOUS AFFAIR
BY ROXANNE ST. CLAIRE

Eldest son Parker Garrison is preoccupied running
his Miami hotel empire and dealing with his recently
deceased father's secret second family. Since he has
little time to date, taking his superefficient assistant
to a charity event should have been a simple plan.
Until passion takes them beyond business.

Don't miss any of the six exciting titles in
THE GARRISONS continuity, beginning in July.
Only from Silhouette Desire.

THE CEO'S SCANDALOUS AFFAIR
#1807

Available July 2007.

REQUEST YOUR FREE BOOKS!
2 FREE NOVELS PLUS 2
FREE GIFTS!

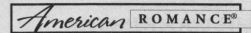 ROMANCE®

Heart, Home & Happiness!

YES! Please send me 2 FREE Harlequin American Romance® novels and my 2 FREE gifts. After receiving them, if I don't wish to receive any more books, I can return the shipping statement marked "cancel." If I don't cancel, I will receive 4 brand-new novels every month and be billed just $4.24 per book in the U.S., or $4.99 per book in Canada, plus 25¢ shipping and handling per book and applicable taxes, if any*. That's a savings of close to 15% off the cover price! I understand that accepting the 2 free books and gifts places me under no obligation to buy anything. I can always return a shipment and cancel at any time. Even if I never buy another book from Harlequin, the two free books and gifts are mine to keep forever.

154 HDN EEZK   354 HDN EEZV

Name _____ (PLEASE PRINT) _____

Address _____ Apt. # _____

City _____ State/Prov. _____ Zip/Postal Code _____

Signature (if under 18, a parent or guardian must sign)

Mail to the **Harlequin Reader Service®:**
IN U.S.A.: P.O. Box 1867, Buffalo, NY 14240-1867
IN CANADA: P.O. Box 609, Fort Erie, Ontario L2A 5X3

Not valid to current Harlequin American Romance subscribers.

Want to try two free books from another line?
Call 1-800-873-8635 or visit www.morefreebooks.com.

* Terms and prices subject to change without notice. NY residents add applicable sales tax. Canadian residents will be charged applicable provincial taxes and GST. This offer is limited to one order per household. All orders subject to approval. Credit or debit balances in a customer's account(s) may be offset by any other outstanding balance owed by or to the customer. Please allow 4 to 6 weeks for delivery.

Your Privacy: Harlequin is committed to protecting your privacy. Our Privacy Policy is available online at www.eHarlequin.com or upon request from the Reader Service. From time to time we make our lists of customers available to reputable firms who may have a product or service of interest to you. If you would prefer we not share your name and address, please check here. ☐

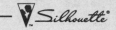

SPECIAL EDITION™

**Look for six new
MONTANA MAVERICKS
stories, beginning in July with**

THE MAN WHO HAD EVERYTHING

by CHRISTINE RIMMER

When Grant Clifton decided to sell the
family ranch, he knew it would devastate
Stephanie Julen, the caretaker who'd always been
like a little sister to him. He wanted a new start,
but how could he tell her that she and her mother
would have to leave...especially now that he was
head over heels in love with her?

MONTANA MAVERICKS

Dreaming big—and winning hearts—in Big Sky Country

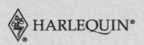

HARLEQUIN®

American ROMANCE®

COMING NEXT MONTH

#1169 THE RANCHER NEXT DOOR by Cathy Gillen Thacker
Texas Legacies: The Carrigans
Rebecca Carrigan expects her alpaca farm will rile the local cattlemen,
especially after she practically steals her property right out from under the
nose of Trevor McCabe. Trevor's interest is definitely piqued by his beautiful
neighbor—and when she is seen on the arm of his archrival, the whole town
knows that's like waving a red flag in front of a bull!

#1170 TROUBLE IN TENNESSEE by Tanya Michaels
In the Family
Treble "Trouble" James isn't thrilled about returning to her hometown of
Joyous, Tennessee, but her sister, pregnant with her first child, needs her.
Thankfully, confronting the people who had judged her youthful, wild behavior
is easier after meeting Dr. Keith Caldwell, a man who has a soft spot for trouble.
Together they create quite a bit of their own!

#1171 HOME TO THE DOCTOR by Mary Anne Wilson
Shelter Island Stories
Holed up to nurse a broken leg, tough-minded businessman Ethan Grace never
expected challenges of any sort at his estate on Shelter Island, in the Pacific
Ocean, off Puget Sound. Then again, he hadn't yet run into now-grown-up lady
doctor Morgan Kelly, smart, beautiful, intriguing—and determined not to let
the powerful Grace conglomerate do her father in...no matter how drawn to
Ethan she is.

#1172 TEMPORARILY TEXAN by Victoria Chancellor
Brody's Crossing
When a mix-up lands gardening consultant Raven York deep in the heart of
Texas cattle country, the strictly vegetarian Yankee is horrified to find herself
bunking down with a meat-eating all-American cowboy. She thinks that tofu is
healthier than a T-bone, but what about the animal attraction she feels for him?

www.eHarlequin.com